UNLIKELY EXPLOITS 1

The Fall of Fergal

or

Not So Dingly In The Dell

When not writing silly books, Philip Ardagh is very serious indeed and frowns a great deal. He also sports a pair of those little round glasses that brainy people often wear. He is best known for the bestselling Eddie Dickens Trilogy, beginning with *Awful End*. *The Fall of Fergal* is the first of his new *Unlikely Exploits* series. He probably lies awake at night thinking: 'Why does no one take me seriously?' His wife is a Doctor of Philosophy, which means that she's far cleverer than he is, but he's bigger than her. So there.

by the same author
published by Faber & Faber

Fiction

Awful End
Book One of the Eddie Dickens Trilogy

Dreadful Acts
Book Two of the Eddie Dickens Trilogy

Non-fiction

The Hieroglyphs Handbook
Teach Yourself Ancient Egyptian

The Archaeologist's Handbook
The Insider's Guide to Digging Up the Past

Did Dinosaurs Snore?
100½ Questions about Dinosaurs Answered

Why Are Castles Castle-Shaped?
100½ Questions about Castles Answered

UNLIKELY EXPLOITS 1

THE FALL OF FERGAL

or

Not So Dingly In The Dell

PHILIP ARDAGH

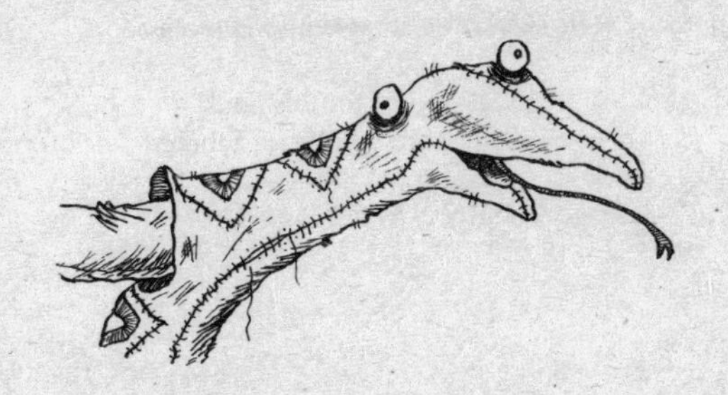

illustrated by David Roberts

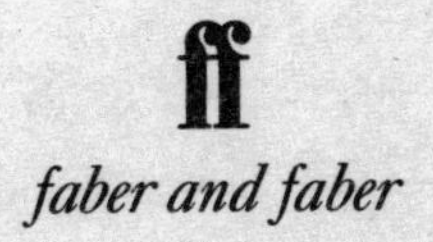

faber and faber

First published in 2002
by Faber and Faber Limited
3 Queen Square, London WC1N 3AU
This paperback edition first published in 2002

Typeset by Faber and Faber Limited
Printed in England by Mackays of Chatham plc, Chatham, Kent

A CIP record for this book
is available from the British Library

ISBN 0–571–21521–1

2 4 6 8 10 9 7 5 3 1

For Rebecca McNally. No relation.
And for my long-departed Great Aunt Phyllis, who gave me one of the greatest gifts of all and never even knew it. Thank you.

A Word to the Wise

There's one thing we need to get straight before any of us get started – me with the writing and you with the reading – and that is this: no matter where you think the events in this book took place, you're wrong. Plain and simple. No room for argument. Just because I have the McNallys speaking English, it doesn't mean they're from an English-speaking country. If you're reading a translated version of the book, it doesn't mean that they actually spoke in the language you're reading either. No. The events in this book took place somewhere none of you has ever been. How can I be sure? Because I'm the author, that's how, and we'll hear no more about it. Discussion closed. And as for the McNallys' names, I know they're strange, but I can't go and change them just to make you happy, now can I? That's what they're called so you'll just have to live with it. In the meantime, I hope you enjoy this, the first of their unlikely exploits.

PHILIP ARDAGH

Marley was dead; to begin with. There is no doubt whatever about that. The register of his burial was signed by the clergyman, the clerk, the undertaker, and the chief mourner . . . Old Marley was as dead as a door nail.

From *A Christmas Carol* by Charles Dickens

Prologue

'Philip!'

What?

'Wake up.'

Huh?

'Wake up! The book's started!'

Started?

'Yes –'

What do you mean, started?

'We've already had the title page, copyright blurb, your "Word to the Wise", the dedication no one ever reads and the quotation.'

You mean . . .?

'Yes, we're on to the story part!'

Blimey.

'You'd better get on with it.'

I'd better.

'Good luck.'

Thanks . . .

Chapter One

The very last words young Fergal McNally heard in his life were: 'Don't lean out of that window!' The very last sounds were probably the air whistling past his sticky-out ears as he fell the fourteen storeys, the honk of traffic horns below (getting nearer and nearer, of course), and – possibly – the 'SP' of the 'SPLAT!' he himself made as he hit the pavement. Fergal certainly wouldn't have heard more than the 'SP', though, because by the time the 'LAT!' part had followed, he would have been well and truly dead.

The person who'd shouted the 'don't-lean-out' warning, good and loud (but far too late), was Fergal's older sister Jackie. Jackie really was an *older*, older sister. Some people (twins, usually) have older sisters just minutes older than them. Lots of people have older sisters a good few years older than them, but Fergal's sister Jackie was old enough to be his mother, which was kind of handy, because he didn't have a real mother. It had been down to Jackie to bring up the rest of them. You know: feed them, clothe them, stop them falling out of windows . . . that kind of thing.

Of course, their father could have brought them up, but he was a useless dad. He even went so far as to get a note from his doctor saying that he was 'excused parenting', and left everything for poor old Jackie to do. He kept himself busy by collecting empty bottles. They were full when he first got them but were certainly empty by the time he'd finished with them. He very rarely spoke to anyone except the man in the bottle shop and to shout at Jackie to tell her how useless she was at everything.

He would hide in what he called 'the back room', though it was more to the side than the back if you counted the front bit of the apartment as being the part that faced the road. He even had his meals in the back room, whilst Jackie fed her brothers and sister (once a day) around a big circular table in the kitchen.

Rufus McNally – that was their father's name – often liked to add to his empty-bottle collection during meal times and would attract Jackie's attention, to bring him another full one, by throwing something at the wall dividing the back room (which was really a side room) from the kitchen. Sometimes it'd be a bottle he'd just emptied. Sometimes it might be a boot. Once he picked up the cat, but Smoky was no fool and, with a few swift strokes of the paw and claw, made it absolutely clear to Captain Rufus that she was by no means a cat of the throwing-across-the-room variety.

You see, Smoky was a working cat, not a pet. She let the McNally children stroke her and she let them love her, but they didn't feed her. (It's not that they were mean, it's just that there was barely enough food for themselves without feeding a cat as well.) Smoky ate the mice and rats that were unwise enough to stop scuttling behind the skirting and make a break across an open floor.

Once Fergal's dad Rufus threw his own wooden leg at the wall to attract Jackie's attention. He'd looked around for something else to throw but couldn't find anything that wasn't furry and purry, so he'd unscrewed his leg and chucked it with such force that it not only cracked the plaster in the wall but also split the leg itself, right along the grain. Thereafter, it always looked like an overripe fruit with a burst skin.

In the days before any of the children (apart from Jackie) had been born, Rufus McNally had been not only a brilliant sailor but also a war hero. He'd been a happy smiling fellow whom – which is simply a 'who' with an 'm' on the end – everyone had been proud to know. He'd been awarded more gold medals for bravery than he had clean shirts to pin the medals on . . . and then he'd lost his leg.

He didn't lose his leg in the way that people lose umbrellas at busy railway stations. No, Captain Rufus McNally lost his leg in such a way that he couldn't simply go to the 'Lost & Found' and collect it. He didn't lose his leg in an explosion, and he'd been in many of those. He didn't lose it when he was clinging to wreckage in shark-infested waters, and he'd found himself in that predicament on more than one occasion. He lost his leg on the fourth occasion he found himself in a sinking ship. On the previous three occasions he'd done heroic deeds to save others trapped as their vessels went down. On this final occasion it was he who was trapped. His ship had been torpedoed by an enemy submarine and was sinking fast, but he was going nowhere because his leg was caught under a mass of twisted metal.

So Captain Rufus McNally did a very brave thing. As the water poured into the cabin where he was trapped, knowing that if he couldn't free himself he would definitely die, he decided to cut off his own leg. Sorry, but there you are. I'd love to say that the solution was to skip happily with fluffy bunnies with nice music in the background, but this was war. And war is a 'orrible thing. If you don't want to know the details, look away until I tell you that it's safe to carry on reading.

Rufus grabbed a razor-sharp piece of twisted metal (that had once been part of a door frame to the boiler room, if you must know) and cut through his leg – and yes, he did have to hack through his own bone – as the rising water around him reddened with his own blood. At the end of it, he fainted but he floated free, and was rescued by some of his own men who'd made it to a lifeboat. They stemmed the bleeding – people never stop the bleeding in war stories, they always 'stem' it – and, fortunately for Rufus, help was close at hand and he survived.

The down side was that he was a changed man. What Rufus McNally went through was unbelievably dreadful – I'd be a liar to tell you otherwise – but other people have been through even worse and somehow come out the other side as decent human beings. Rufus McNally, however, became bitter, sick and twisted – in that order (he'd tried twisted, bitter and sick but it didn't suit) – and it was then that he started to d-r-i-n–

Oh, hang on. I almost forgot:

IT'S OK TO START READING AGAIN, YOU SQUEAMISH ONES.

From being a popular hero, Rufus turned his back on all his old friends and colleagues and wanted to be alone. He had his war pension and, whenever he needed a bit more money, he'd have his wife (and, after she died, Jackie) sell another of his many medals. Poor Jackie. That was just another one of her jobs. No wonder she got a bit snappy sometimes.

Fergal and the other kids – his twin brothers Joshua and Albie and his sister Le Fay – sometimes called Jackie 'Jackal', which may have seemed a bit mean. Wouldn't you snap and snarl, once in a while, with four younger siblings to look after and no life of your own? Probably. Although there may, of course, have been more to her name than that. Those of you who read on shall see.

But I'm pretty sure they all loved each other. In fact, I'd go so far as to say that I expect Jackie, Joshua, Albie and Le Fay (or, if you'd prefer them in alphabetical order: Albie, Jackie, Joshua and Le Fay) were really upset when their little brother Fergal ended up all dead like that. SPLAT!

The sad thing was that things were looking up for the McNally family at the time Fergal took a nosedive from the window. For a start, it was a hotel window from which Fergal fell and – although Fergal's other sister, Le Fay, was the only person who was supposed to be occupying the hotel room (it was a 'single') – they'd never been in the position before in which even *one* of them could legitimately spend the night in a hotel. And The Dell was quite a posh one. Le Fay had entered a typing competition and had won her local and regional finals. Now she was in the national grand finals and that meant a trip to the capital and a night in The Dell.

What is a typing competition? you may well ask. Well, although I've never actually been in one myself, because I can only type with two fingers, I think you'll find it's a competition to see who can type the fastest, making the fewest mistakes whilst still laying all the words neatly on the page – that kind of thing. Now, it may not sound the most exciting thing to you. You may think that a kick-boxing competition or a fight with laser swords, or a motorbike competition might be more interesting, but it was a typing competition Le Fay had entered and reached the finals in, and there's nothing I can do to change that. Anyhow, her brothers and sisters were very proud of her.

Of course, their father wasn't in the least bit proud of her or her typing abilities. (It wasn't the typing part. He wouldn't have been in the least bit proud if Le Fay had run a mile in under one second or performed successful brain surgery on three patients all at once, either. He was excused being a parent, remember. All he cared about was himself.)

When Le Fay asked if she could go to the grand finals – she hadn't told him about the locals or regionals – he said that he didn't care what she did. When Jackie suggested that the rest of them go with Le Fay to give her support, their father said he wasn't going anywhere and, if he wasn't going anywhere, none of the others was going anywhere either.

So Jackie made a stand. She was a grown woman, old enough to be Fergal's mother, and had looked after all of them, including her father, long enough to make an important decision on her own. She took the money she'd been putting aside from her already meagre housekeeping budget each week – the plan had been to save up enough money to buy the others a small present each, come Christmas – and found that she had enough to buy just two return coach tickets to the capital.

Le Fay would be travelling up to town by train at the expense of Tap 'n' Type, the sponsors of the typing competition, but there was no way Jackie could afford to buy two train tickets. The two coach tickets were for her and for Albie and Joshua. The reason why Albie and Joshua only got one ticket between them was that they were almost-identical twins. Jackie hoped that if they kept on the move and took it in turns to hide in the loo, the coach driver would think that they were one and the same person. That left Fergal without a ticket. There were two options here. They could either hide him in their luggage, or dress him up as a baby so that he could travel for nothing.

When the time came, Fergal found himself in the coach on Jackie's lap, with a big nappy (which is a diaper, only spelled n-a-p-p-y instead of d-i-a-p-e-r) on his bottom, and a Sherlock Holmes comic book in his hand.

Sitting next to them, a man with a moustache eyed Fergal's reading material. 'Bright kid,' he said. The moustache said nothing.

Although the coach left two hours before the train, it was due to arrive an hour and a half after it, so Le Fay arranged to meet them at the back of The Dell at three o'clock in the afternoon. There was no way Jackie, Fergal, Albie and Joshua could simply march into the building with their luggage, even if Fergal was pretending to be a baby and Albie and Joshua were pretending to be one and the same person. The management of The Dell would suspect that there was something funny going on (funny peculiar, not funny ha-ha). No,

Le Fay would have to find a way of smuggling them up to her room.

Le Fay had been met at the station by a man called Malcolm (which, by the way, is the name of a stuffed stoat in another series of books I wrote, starting with *Awful End*, which I'd be very grateful if you'd rush out and buy). Malcolm Kent was from the publicity department of Tap 'n' Type and it was his job to meet the four finalists off their four respective trains.

'You're the last,' Malcolm explained, taking Le Fay's rather tatty-looking suitcases. Old suitcases in novels are nearly always battered. This was tatty. (The piece of cod the McNallys shared later that evening was definitely battered, though, so you fans of battering have nothing to fear.) 'The other finalists are already back at the hotel.'

Malcolm had a taxi waiting and he held the door open for Le Fay to get into the back. Le Fay had never been in the capital before, had never been in a taxi before and had never stayed in a hotel before. This, she thought, as she settled down in the comfy seat, is going to be a trip to remember. It was, but sadly for the wrong reason. This was going to be the trip where Fergal ended up very squashed and very dead.

Chapter Two

When Malcolm Kent had first laid eyes on Le Fay McNally – which was at the railway/railroad/train station, because he hadn't been at her local or regional heat of the competition – he'd been rather surprised by her appearance.

With the exception of mentioning Fergal's sticky-out ears, I haven't really paid much attention to describing what everyone looked like. You'll see why in a moment. You already know that Dad McNally – Cap'n Rufus – had a wooden leg, and you already know that Albie and Joshua were almost identical, but what you probably didn't know until now is that they all had wiry, untameable gingery-red hair and they all had freckles – hundreds of them in all. And all of them – the McNallys, not the freckles – had two large front teeth with a gap between them except for

Jackie 'the Jackal'. Hers looked more like George Washington's, which, I believe, were actually made of wood. In other words, once you've described one McNally you've just about described them all . . . and none of them was about to win any beauty contests; but then again, if you've seen my author photograph, you'll be fully aware that neither am I. Their father looked the most unlike the others because of his big red nose. He hadn't always had a big red nose and it wasn't something that he could pass on to his children. In other words, it wasn't hereditary and had more to do with his trips to the bottle shop.

But it wasn't Le Fay's buck teeth, unmanageable hair and multiple freckles that surprised Malcolm from Tap 'n' Type. It wasn't how shabby her clothes were and how unwashed she looked. (Jackie did her best, but there was no running water in their apartment except for a drip from the ceiling from the apartment upstairs and the condensation on the windows in cold weather.) What shocked Malcolm was how thin and how hungry she looked.

Now, Malcolm wasn't the most caring man in the world. He never gave money to charity, not even to those nice ones that look after unwanted donkeys or retired pit ponies that have been down the mines all their working lives. He didn't always hold doors open for senior citizens and, on more than one occasion, he had smoked in a no-smoking waiting room at a railway station.

Once – and I checked this with his parents, who swear that it is true – he didn't even bother to thank his gran for the socks and aftershave she gave him one Christmas. But when Malcolm first laid eyes on Le Fay McNally, he hoped beyond hope that she would win the grand final of the Tap 'n' Type typing competition.

He thought of the three other finalists: Graham Large, Peggy Snoot and Anna Malting. Graham Large had arrived with three pieces of very expensive-looking matching luggage, and his parents had paid extra so that he could travel down first class and have a whole suite of rooms – separate bedroom, bathroom and sitting room – in The Dell instead of a single room. He'd bossed Malcolm around as though he was a personal servant, not a representative of the sponsors.

Peggy Snoot was nice enough. Very polite, in fact. She seemed a little nervous, but why not? The finals were important to all the contestants.

Anna Malting was a different matter altogether. In the taxi from the station to the hotel she'd gone on and on and on about how her local and regional heats in the competition had been so much harder than everyone else's, and what she was going to do *when* she won the grand prize, not *if*.

Large, Snoot and Malting all looked well dressed, well cared for and well fed. Not Le Fay McNally. Malcolm crossed his fingers and, though he wasn't a religious man, muttered a little prayer to God just in case He (or, of course, She) existed.

Once Malcolm had shown Le Fay to her room, he showed her the itinerary. If you've no idea what an itinerary is, you might imagine that it was a wonderful machine made of gleaming chrome, with horns to shout down and earpieces to listen into. If the truth be told, the itinerary was a piece of paper with type printed on it. Being the itinerary for:

The Grand Finals of
The Young Typist of the Year
sponsored by Tap 'n' Type
Providers of Keyboards to the
Crowned Heads of Europe & Beyond

it was beautifully typed!

Her heart thumping, Le Fay read it quickly to make sure that she'd be able to meet Jackie, Albie, Joshua and Fergal outside The Dell at three o'clock as originally planned. She didn't have a watch. (The McNallys couldn't afford one, and her arms were so thin one would probably have slipped right off over her hand anyway.)

There was to be a 'Meet the Other Finalists' at a 'finger buffet' in the Bellhop Suite at one o'clock. Le Fay knew what a buffet was. There had been a buffet car on the train. A buffet meant food, which suited her fine. If she was really smart, she might come up with a way of snaffling some of the buffet to give to the others when they arrived.

It was the 'finger' part that bothered her a bit. Would all the food be fingers? She could think of fish fingers, and there was a plant called ochre, which some people called 'ladies' fingers', but she couldn't think of any other kinds of fingers people might eat. Then she remembered Jackie telling her that there was a delicious pudding called trifle, which had sponge fingers in it. At least those kinds of fingers sounded OK!

The next item on the itinerary was two o'clock, 'Meet the Press', described as being 'A Photo Call with some of the Capital City's Leading Evening Newspapers'.

Le Fay hoped that this wouldn't take more than an hour, because after that it was 'A Free Afternoon for Sightseeing' right up until 'Dinner with our Generous Sponsors in the Sizzle Grill' at eight o'clock . . . which would leave her with plenty of time to spend with her family.

'You don't have to wait until lunch or supper to have some food,' said Malcolm kindly. 'You can use Room Service any time you want.'

'What's that, please?' Le Fay asked politely.

'If you, say, want a chicken sandwich or a mug of hot chocolate,' said Malcolm, 'you pick up that phone, dial 1 and tell them what you want. They bring it to your room and you sign for it, but you don't have to pay. Tap 'n' Type pays. See?'

'I see,' said Le Fay, wide-eyed in wonderment. She imagined people throughout the hotel picking up their phones and ordering chicken and hot chocolate! It was like living in a palace.

This is another example of Malcolm Kent being a very nice man at heart. Room Service was not something officially offered as part of the grand finalists' trip. Of course, Graham Large could dial up and order what he wanted, but Mummy and Daddy would be sent the bill at the end of his stay. Peggy Snoot was far too polite to even think of ringing for Room Service, because Malcolm hadn't told her she could; and when Anna Malting had said: 'I can call down for anything I want, can't I? After all, I've earned it,' Malcolm had replied: 'I'm afraid you will be charged for it, though phone calls home are free.'

'You can ring home too, of course,' Malcolm now told Le Fay. 'You dial 9 for an outside line and then your number.'

'Thank you,' said Le Fay. She didn't want to disappoint the nice man from Tap 'n' Type by telling him that they didn't have a phone at home. They'd used to have one, but the telephone company had got fed up coming to repair the wiring every time her father tore the phone out of the wall and threw it across the back room (which was really at the side).

'Right,' said Malcolm. 'So it's dial 1 for Room Service–'

'And 9 for an outside line,' Le Fay nodded.

'Both the Bellhop Suite and the Sizzle Grill are here in The Dell,' said Malcolm. 'They're both on the first floor. Follow the signs.'

'Thank you.'

'I'll see you at the "Meet the Other Finalists" then, OK?' said Malcolm. 'But feel free to call up Room Service before then if you're hungry.'

'Chicken sandwich and a mug of hot chocolate,' Le Fay nodded. 'Thanks.'

Malcolm went out through the open doorway and closed the door to Le Fay's room behind him. She was alone at last. Now she would have to come up with a way of smuggling the rest of the McNallys inside.

If she'd failed, of course, little Fergal might still be living a normal life today.

Chapter Three

The ambulance man took one look at what was left of Fergal and knew that there would be no driving to the Sacred Heart Hospital at breakneck speed with lights flashing and sirens blaring. The neck-breaking had already happened and, once the doctor had officially declared the poor boy dead – something that anyone with a pair of eyes in his or her head could have done at a glance – he'd simply wait for the police photographer to take a few photographs then scoop the kid into a body bag and take a leisurely drive to the morgue.

The morgue was another name for the mortuary. It was in the basement of the Sacred Heart Hospital, where they put the bodies of those who'd died in the hospital or were brought in dead from outside: accident and murder victims.

The ambulance man, whose name was Morris, idly wondered whether Fergal (though at that stage, of course, he didn't know that the victim's name was Fergal) was the victim of an accident or murder . . . or even suicide? Sometimes people deliberately jumped out of windows. Did this one fall, was he pushed or did he jump?

The doctor – a roundish man who looked, walked and spoke remarkably like a duck – arrived, waddled quacking through the small crowd that had gathered, nodded at one of the uniformed police officers keeping people at a respectful distance, and knelt down next to Fergal.

He whistled through his teeth. 'Fell twelve floors?' he guessed.

'Fourteen,' said the assistant manager of The Dell, a small man with greased-back black hair and a moustache so thin that it looked as if it'd been drawn with one of those extra-fine-nibbed drawing pens. His name was Mr Lesley, spelled the girl's way.

The doctor cursed under his breath. 'I used to be accurate to within one storey,' he muttered, getting to his feet. 'He's dead all right!' he called out to Morris. 'Bag him and tag him.'

Mr Lesley cleared his throat purposefully. It's amazing what message a purposeful clearing of the throat can convey. This one could be instantly translated into: 'Show a bit more respect, doc. The victim's grieving family are within earshot'; and within earshot they certain were.

The moment Fergal had toppled out of the window, Jackie had dashed across the room and leant out, grabbing at thin air. She had let out a cry of 'No!', stretching the 'o' to last a good fifteen seconds, but it's no good me writing it down as 'Noooooooooooooooo!' because that looks as though it rhymes with 'moo' – the noise cartoon cows make – and is the noise Scottish folk make in very bad Hollywood films. This was very definitely a 'no!' to rhyme with 'snow', with the 'ow' long-drawn-out and distraught. It should also be added to the list of the last sounds Fergal probably heard on his way to his squishy death. I'm sorry, I should have thought of it earlier and I hope you don't feel that I've betrayed you as a narrator. Well, at least I've apologised.

Those smart alecs amongst you who are wondering why I didn't mention Fergal's own screaming as he fell fourteen storeys, I simply tell you this: I made no mention of Fergal's scream because he didn't scream or cry as he fell. He fell as silently as a sack of rocks, or potatoes, or something equally silent. Perhaps it was the shock of it all. Perhaps he was about to scream when he came into contact with the solid ground, and all thought of screaming went out of his mind . . .

There, now look what you've made me go and

do: get all involved in the unpleasant side of things again. Where was I? Yes, Jackie had dashed to the window and, seeing that it was too late to catch him, ran straight to the door and out into the corridor.

Le Fay, Albie and Joshua dashed out of the hotel room after their big sister, who'd already reached the lift and was jumping up to press the 'down' button. There were two lifts and, according to the arrow indicator above them, one was on the ninety-third floor and the other on the forty-sixth.

Jackie headed for the main stairs and ran down them at an incredible speed, sobbing as she went, jumping five or six steps at a time. Le Fay, Albie and Joshua somehow managed to keep up, all sobbing their eyes out.

Nothing funny happened at this stage so, if you're hoping for a laugh, we interrupt this story for a joke. Now it's not original, it's not my joke and I'm not claiming it as my own. It's simply the first joke that came into my head when I thought that a little levity might be in order:

Two cannibals are eating a boiled clown. One cannibal turns to the other, between mouthfuls, and says: 'Does this taste funny to you?' Ho ho!

There. Not a side-splitter, but it certainly brought a twitch of a smile to the corners of my mouth and is a nice relief from all those sobbing relatives of Fergal McNally charging downstairs to what was a foregone conclusion: one splatted little brother.

Anyway, I think I'm getting rather ahead of myself again. When we left Le Fay at the end of Chapter Two, she hadn't even smuggled her family into her room, so Fergal can't have had the opportunity to fall out of the window yet. Perhaps we should go back a bit . . .

*

On the back of Le Fay's door were two framed notices, both printed entirely in red ink. One was headed: IN THE EVENT OF HOLES and the other: IN THE EVENT OF FIRE. The one headed: IN THE EVENT OF HOLES was full of doom and gloom and basically said that, if a huge hole opened up under the hotel, there wasn't a great deal you could do except hide under your bed and pray or stand in the doorway. Ideally both: hide under your bed in the doorway and pray. Le Fay was of the opinion that if a big hole opened up under the hotel, no matter what you did, you'd still end up in it.

It was the second notice – IN THE EVENT OF FIRE – in equally red print, that caught her eye. It gave useful tips about not using the lifts and where the 'assembly point' was so that management could do a roll call and try to work out who was still trapped in the building and needed rescuing.

There was a drawing too. It was a plan of the floor of the hotel her room was on and, as well as the main stairs, it showed some back stairs marked: DOWN TO FIRE EXIT. If these stairs led down from her floor to the fire exit, Le Fay reasoned, then they must also lead *up* from the fire exit to her floor! She would go and investigate.

Slipping her room key, with its long metal tag, into the only pocket of her best (but still very drab) dress, she slipped out of her room, along the corridor to the left and slipped through a door marked: FIRE EXIT. (Yup, there was suddenly a lot of slipping, but not of the 'oops!' banana-skin variety.)

It opened on to a cold, dark staircase of uncarpeted concrete steps with a metal handrail set into the wall; a real contrast to the posh plushness of the rest of The Dell. The stairs seemed to go back on themselves in a spiral square – if there is such a thing as a spiral square – for ever and ever (with fire-exit doors from each floor leading on to them); but, finally, Le Fay reached the bottom. There was a set of double doors with a metal bar running across them at average-adult-waist height. EMERGENCY EXIT ONLY, said the sign. PUSH BAR.

It was obvious to Le Fay that there wouldn't be any handles on the outside of the door, which, from the smell of exhaust fumes and honking of car horns, she guessed opened out on to the street, probably at the side of the hotel. This was to stop people doing exactly what Le Fay's family planned to do: sneak in without paying. The only way to get Jackie, Fergal, Albie and Joshua inside this way was to open the door, somehow keep it wedged open, then circle the hotel with them until they found it . . . but what if someone found the exit wedged open first? That's why Le Fay decided she wouldn't open it there and then, but leave it until just before three o'clock, when she'd arranged to meet the others. Le Fay went all the way back up the fourteen storeys via the back stairs.

She could, of course, have slipped out through any of the fire doors and taken the lift up the rest of the way, but she didn't want to arouse suspicion. For all she knew, big hotels such as The Dell hired detectives to be on the lookout for strange goings-on, twenty-four hours a day; and Le Fay was right about that, as you will discover. They're called 'house detectives' and the chief house detective at The Dell was a man named Charlie Tweedy. Charlie was to become interested in the McNally children – very interested indeed.

But Le Fay had no way of knowing that. Not then.

Charlie was an ex-naval man and an ex-policeman and, in all the time he'd been on the force, he'd never let an unsolved case remain unsolved. He was like a terrier, which is one of those dogs that, once it's sunk its teeth into you, won't let go until it's well and truly satisfied it's 'won'.

If you don't believe me, you should see my brother's nose. He bent down to pat a terrier once and to say 'Nice doggie', or whatever it is that brothers say to terriers; but the dog took it to mean 'Let's fight!' When my brother stood up, he had the dog attached to his nose . . . It would probably still be there today if the dog's owner hadn't shown it something more tasty to chew on. My brother does still have a faint scar to remember the occasion, though.

If I told you Charlie had a nickname, you might, therefore, expect it to be along the lines of 'Terrier Tweedy'. That's certainly the name I would have given him. But no, Charlie Tweedy was known in the trade as 'Twinkle-Toes' Tweedy. Stick around long enough, and you'll find out why.

Back inside her room, and a bit out of breath from running down the back stairs and up again, Le Fay looked at the time on the radio alarm clock on the bedside table: 12:18.

Le Fay was feeling very hungry by now, which wasn't unusual, because she was used to having only one (rather small) main meal a day back home, but she wondered whether she should ring Room Service and ask for a chicken sandwich and a mug of hot chocolate. Sure, it was less than three-quarters of an hour until she was supposed to be eating fingers in the Sizzle Grill – or was it the Bellhop Suite? – but the more she thought about plates piled high with fingers, the less appetising the whole 'Meet the Other Contestants' seemed. What if they were monkey fingers? They'd look almost human . . . and would the nails have been taken off, or were you supposed to peel them off yourself? Or was it polite to eat them? They'd be very crunchy.

Le Fay McNally picked up the phone and dialled the number '1'.

'Room Service,' said a cheery voice.

'I'd like a chicken sandwich and a mug of chocolate, please,' said Le Fay.

'Certainly, madam,' said the cheery voice. 'White, brown or rye?'

'A chicken sandwich and a mug of chocolate, please,' Le Fay repeated, a little less sure of herself this time.

'The bread, madam. For the sandwich. Would you like white bread, brown bread or rye bread?'

'Oh!' said Le Fay, relieved. 'White, please.'

'Toasted?'

'Yes. Yes, please. And a mug of hot chocolate.'

'Certainly, madam. One toasted chicken sandwich on white and a mug of hot chocolate for Room 1428. It'll be with you within fifteen minutes,' said the cheery voice.

'Thank you,' said Le Fay. 'Goodbye, then.'

'Goodbye, dear,' said Room Service.

Le Fay put the phone down and sat on the bed. How had Room Service known which room she was in? she wondered. Were there cameras in all the rooms to make sure that people didn't steal the soap or something? If there were cameras all over the hotel, then she'd have been seen slipping through the fire-exit door and they'd probably want to know why . . .

No, Le Fay told herself. She was just being silly.

There must be some way that the telephone system in Room Service could tell which room you were dialling from. It must light up a number, or something. That's what it must be. She was being stupid. Who'd stay in a hotel with hidden cameras everywhere? All the guests would be embarrassed and go to bed with their clothes on.

Back home, she and Jackie, Fergal, Albie and Joshua often went to bed with their clothes on in the winter, but not because they didn't want people filming them in the nude. They did it because it was far too cold to take their clothes off at night. In fact, they'd often put on extra clothes – including the odd coat or two – before settling down to sleep. Another way of trying to keep warm was all to sleep in the same bed, which is what they did.

Since their mother had died, their father slept in the back room (which was really a side room, remember), but he had the one-bar electric heater on all night in the cold months, so he was fine. The rest of them bundled into what had once been his double bed and snuggled up together as best they could. Le Fay was the one who always felt the cold most and, despite layers of shirts and coats, often kept Jackie awake with her teeth chattering.

Five minutes later, there was a knock at the door.

'Room Service!' said a voice.

Le Fay jumped off the bed and opened the door.

It wasn't Room Service at all.

'Are you Le Fay McNally?' asked a complete stranger, with a very unpleasant sneer indeed.

Chapter Four

Framed in the doorway of Room 1428 of The Dell hotel at 12:33 that day was a very large boy wearing a rather tight navy-blue shirt (with monogrammed pocket) and an equally-tight pair of dark blue shorts that reached the tops of his knees. The lower parts of his legs were covered with a pair of white socks, with navy-blue piping, that reached the *bottom* of his knees.

His face was a little podgy and the skin looked so soft that Le Fay imagined that it must have been bathed in twenty-three different lotions and then had thirteen different creams massaged into it with loving care. (She was wrong: it was twenty-four different lotions.) But it was the hair – my God, the hair – that was most shocking of all. Thick, dark brown and swept back into an enormous quiff, it was so stiff that it looked more like spun sugar. How long, Le Fay wondered, did it take to get your hair to look like that each morning? And, even more to the point, *why*? She couldn't take her eyes off the top of his head. She'd never met such a sweet-smelling, softy-skinned, quiffy person in shorts before!

'You must be McNally, the poor girl,' said the boy, pushing past her and walking uninvited into her room. 'I see they've put you in one of the cheapest rooms. More of a closet really, isn't it?' He wrinkled his nose as though he'd just detected a particularly bad smell. 'I'm Graham Large,' he said, which was true. 'I'm the one who's going to beat you all in the competition tomorrow,' he added, sounding rather too sure of himself. 'My father is David Large, owner of Large Lunches. I expect you've heard of him.'

'Er, no,' said Le Fay, politely.

Graham had been looking to see whether Le Fay had brought a typewriter or laptop with her to practise on and, concluding that she'd brought next to nothing with her – let alone a keyboard – turned and stared at her.

If you were to ask Le Fay what colours his eyes were, she wouldn't remember. He may have been glaring directly at her face, but her eyes were still fixed on the h-a-i-r.

'Sponsors always like to have a poor person in the finals of a competition, whatever it's for,' said

Graham Large, with that nasty, nasty sneer that came naturally. 'They fix local and regional competitions to make sure it happens. It makes them look a kind, caring company . . . but there's no way the poor kid ever wins. How could you? You didn't get this far on talent or merit. It's just rigged so that you can make up the numbers.'

Le Fay was confused. Firstly, she didn't see herself as being poor and, secondly, she knew that she had excellent keyboard skills.

'We're not poor,' she said, thinking of her friend Simon.

Simon was so poor that he couldn't afford another name. He was simply 'Simon'– as opposed to 'Simple Simon', the guy who met a pie man – and he lived with his family in an old abandoned greenhouse on some wasteland near the edge of Fishbone Forest. (Only someone very poor or completely mad would go anywhere near Fishbone Forest, let alone live near there. It was the sort of place you'd go to if you had absolutely nowhere else to go. Strange things happened in Fishbone Forest – nasty things. The kind of things that people write about in books, such as the next one in this series: *Heir of Mystery*.) Now, Simon and his family were really poor.

Graham Large snorted. It was a contemptuous snort, but don't worry if you're not sure what contemptuous means. It was a piggy snort too. 'If you say so,' he laughed. 'Though why anyone who wasn't poor would turn up dressed in those rags escapes me!'

Now, it was true that Le Fay's dress had been Jackie's dress before she'd grown out of it and that it had been their mother's before Jackie's, but it'd been new when their mother had bought it, so it was less of a handed-down hand-me-down than *some* of the clothes Le Fay wore. It was also true that it'd had a number of alterations and repairs done on it over the years, but Jackie had gone to a great deal of trouble to unpick and re-stitch some of the messier efforts at patching it up, and Le Fay wasn't about to let some perfumed softy make fun of all the hard work her sister had gone to to make her look nice for the competition.

Le Fay had gone red in the face. Her blood was boiling and she was about to . . . about to EXPLODE. What she meant to say next was: 'Get out of my room, Large! I didn't invite you in here!' What she actually said in her spluttering rage was: 'Get out of my room, Lard!' and then spluttered to a halt. Why? Because of the boy's expression the second the word 'Lard' came out.

A look of horror crossed Graham Large's softy, perfumed face. His spun-sugar quiff quivered (quiffs do that sometimes; perhaps that's how they got the name). His eyes – whatever colour they were – moistened. What Le Fay didn't realise was that 'Lard' – her slip of the tongue – was the nickname Graham Large hated most in the whole wide world. It was the name the other boys and girls had used to chant at school before his parents had taken him out of the schooling system and hired a non-teasing, one-on-one private tutor to teach him at home.

'You,' he said, sweeping past Le Fay (with a trail of scent) and striding into the corridor, 'have just made yourself a powerful enemy! A very powerful one!' which was followed by a large sniff.

No sooner had Le Fay shut the door, with some satisfaction, it must be admitted, than there was another knock on it.

'Yes?' she said.

'Room Service!' said a voice.

This time Le Fay went up on tiptoe and looked through the seeing-eye to see who was out there. Through the distorted fish-eye lens, she could see a man in a red uniform with big brass buttons holding a silver tray. She opened the door excitedly.

The young man brought in a delicious-smelling toasted-chicken sandwich on white bread, and a steaming mug of hot chocolate on the tray, which he placed on the bed.

'Thank you,' said Le Fay and, when the man handed her a piece of paper, she signed it with the pen he offered her. 'Thank you very much.'

It was one of the best meals that Le Fay had ever had; and did she feel guilty that she was eating it without Jackie and the others? No, because once she'd smuggled them up there, they could all order as many chicken sandwiches and mugs of hot chocolate as they wanted!

Just before one o'clock, when Le Fay was hurrying to the Bellhop Suite for the first event on the Tap 'n' Type itinerary, Jackie (holding Fergal dressed as a baby) and Albie and Joshua (doing their best to look like one and the same person) were climbing off the coach along with all the other passengers. It wasn't that they'd reached their destination. Far from it. They were on a very, very long fenced road, which appeared to be in the middle of nowhere, with fields on either side, stretching far into the distance, without a single house or turn-off in sight. And there, in front of them, was a hole in the road. A big one.

This wasn't one of those holes in the road that you can drive over and everyone in the car feels funny in the pit of his/her stomach. This was the kind of hole that, if the coach driver attempted to drive over it, he would actually end up driving the coach into, and everyone would end up screaming 'Aaaaargh!' – except, perhaps, for Fergal, who (hindsight tells us) was prone to be as silent as a sack of rocks when falling any great distance – as they plummeted in the general direction of the centre of the Earth, with a capital 'E'.

The coach driver was attempting to lean over the edge of the hole to get an idea of just how deep it was, but was too frightened to get close enough to the edge to get a proper look.

'It weren't there this mornin',' he kept on saying.

The hole in the road can't have been there that long because there wasn't much of a queue of traffic in either direction. The coach was only three vehicles away from it, and there was only a handful of cars the other side of the hole, facing in the opposite direction. A wisp of black smoke drifted out of the hole and hung in the air like a sooty question mark.

'Who do you think made it?' Albie asked Jackie. He'd heard about such holes appearing out of nowhere, but never actually seen one before. He was running around Joshua in circles, in the hope that, if he kept moving, they might have the appearance of being one person with a blurred outline. The actual effect was of one of a pair of almost-identical twins running around the other.

'Who or *what*, my boy,' said the man with the moustache who'd been sitting next to Jackie throughout the journey,

'You mean aliens?' gasped Albie.

'I wish I knew. These holes have been springing up everywhere these past six months. No one seems to know why or how.' Once again, his moustache said nothing.

In keeping with pretending to be a baby, to avoid needing a ticket to travel, Fergal crawled on all-fours to the edge of the gigantic hole and peered into the vast nothingness below.

'Careful!' called Jackie, running after him.

'It's a long way down,' Fergal whispered.

'It weren't there this mornin',' said the coach driver. (I did mention he kept on saying that.)

'How do you propose to get us across, driver?' demanded a grey-haired woman passenger.

'We ain't never gettin' across that, lady,' he said.

'But we've a typing competition to get to!' said Jackie urgently. The man with the moustache eyed her with interest, but said nothing.

'And I am due to be matron of honour at a wedding!' said the grey-haired woman, indignantly.

'Well, it weren't there this mornin',' said the coach driver. If he'd been wearing a cap, I'm sure he'd have taken it off and scratched his head, but he wasn't, so he didn't.

'Then we must get around it,' Fergal blurted out, because he knew how important it was to Le Fay to have her family there to cheer her on.

The man with the moustache appeared at Jackie's side. 'Really bright kid,' he commented.

The driver who'd also heard the super-baby's comment shook his head. 'There's no way that I can get this coach around the edge of the hole,' he said. 'Who knows how soft the earth is in them fields? The whole thing might sink with us in it!'

'We could all wait until you'd driven around it and get back in afterwards,' the grey-haired woman suggested. 'That way the coach would be much lighter.'

'But I still might sink in it,' muttered the driver. 'There ain't no way I'm drivin' around it and that's final, missus!'

'Maybe not,' said the man with the moustache, 'but we can all walk round and try to hitch a ride off the people in the cars the other side. There's nothing they can do except turn back the way they came, anyhow.'

'A brilliant idea!' said Jackie. 'Can you unload our luggage, please, driver?'

While one group of passengers peered into the amazing hole, another argued with the coach driver to let them have their luggage. It wasn't easy.

'I'm only authorised to open the luggage

compartment and release luggage at the end of a journey, see?' he explained, making life difficult for everyone.

'But surely there are special rules for if there's an accident?' asked Jackie.

'Exactly!' said the grey-haired woman. 'Now get on with it, my good man. I've a wedding to attend.'

'But there hasn't been an accident,' the driver protested.

'There would have been if you hadn't stopped in time,' said Jackie.

'But there's nothing in the rules about unloading the luggage if an accident's been avoided,' whined the driver.

'Are there any other circumstances when you're allowed to release the luggage?' asked the man with the moustache, 'apart from when reaching our destination or in the event of an accident, I mean?'

'In the event of a breakdown,' said the driver.

'So, if the coach won't go, then you can let us have our luggage?' asked Albie, coming to a halt in his orbit around Joshua.

'If suitable alternat–' began the driver, but Albie and Joshua weren't listening, they were already sprinting over to the coach.

'Well, technically speaking, what with the queue

of cars now forming behind us and two cars and a huge hole in front, this coach can't go anywhere, now can it?' Jackie McNally asked politely.

'That's as maybe,' said the driver, 'but there's a difference between a car breaking down and–'

'Ah!' said the man with the moustache as a thought suddenly struck him. 'What if the coach was stuck in a patch of mud? The engine was working perfectly and everything, just that the wheels were slipping in the mud and the coach was going nowhere?'

The driver paused, then a smile slowly spread across his face. 'Then I'd probably unload the luggage . . . even though the coach itself ain't reached its destination, been in an accident nor broken down!'

'Exactly!' said the man, triumphantly.

'Which is the same as what's 'appened 'ere!' declared the coach driver.

'Exactly!' said Jackie, the man with the moustache, the grey-haired woman and Fergal-in-his-nappy, all together.

'Then let's get unloading!' declared the driver, striding towards his machine, just as Albie and Joshua McNally appeared from the other side of the coach, looking sheepish.

To anyone viewing Albie and Joshua front on, he or she'd only be able to tell that *Joshua* was looking sheepish, because Albie was standing directly behind him, flat against him, to create the impression of one double-thick human being, requiring just one ticket, rather than that of two almost-identical twins. At least that was the idea.

'You've got a flat tyre, mister,' Joshua told the driver. 'This coach is going nowhere.'

The driver let out a loud and multi-toned groan (surprisingly like the sound a set of half-inflated bagpipes might make if you sat on them, expelling the remaining air) and hurried off to investigate.

When she thought no one was looking, Jackie prodded Joshua in the ribs. 'He was going to unload the luggage anyway,' she said in a harsh whisper.

'But we didn't know that, did we?' came Albie's voice from the back of Joshua's head. 'And it's not as if we did anything to the engine or anything.'

'True,' Jackie agreed and smiled.

Not ten minutes later, Jackie, Albie and Joshua were skirting around the very large, very deep hole with the man with the moustache. Jackie was carrying Fergal, to keep up the pretence for the time being, Joshua and Albie were carrying their trunk between them and, as well as his own small suitcase (which he referred to as his valise), the man with the moustache carried the McNally's other case. The moustache carried nothing.

If something's funny once, it's funny a thousand times – as my Cousin Claire said the day the Iapohani Indians buried her alive to prevent her telling them any more knock-knock jokes – but you'll hear no more jokes about this man-with-a-moustache's moustache! Honestly. Perhaps it would be easier if I gave you his name, and now's an appropriate time because it was just about now that he told it to Jackie.

'My name's Peach, by the way,' he said.

'We're the McNallys,' said Jackie. 'I'm Jackie–'

'And I'm her brother Fergal and I'm not really a baby!' said Fergal, 'so you can put me down now, Jacks.'

Jackie stopped and put her little brother down.

'And we're two almost-identical twins, Albie and Joshua,' said Albie.

'I'm Joshua,' said Albie.

'And I'm Albie,' said Joshua. 'And we're not really one and the same person at all.'

'I never doubted it for a second,' said Mr Peach politely.

They continued skirting the edge of the hole. (It was a large one, remember.) Now that she had her hands free, Jackie insisted that she carry her own case, but Peach insisted that he continue to carry it for her.

Fergal dropped back behind the others and peered into the hole again. What on Earth could have made such a thing? Had it been something from above, or something from below? Whatever it was, Fergal was very glad that it hadn't opened up just as the coach had been driving over that very spot. He hoped that no one else had been driving over that spot at the time . . .

Fergal stopped in his tracks. He felt sure that he'd heard something.

'Ssssh!' he said.

Jackie carried on talking to Mr Peach, and Albie to Joshua.

'SHHHH!' he said, in capital letters this time. They SHHHH!-ed.

'Help,' said a strange and tiny voice.

Fergal gasped. 'I think it's coming from down there!' He pointed.

Chapter Five

Mr Peach grinned. It must have been a very large grin, because it even showed under his big moustache.

'Forgive me,' he said. 'I was pulling your leg.'

'What do you mean?' asked Fergal.

'Peter Piper picked a peck of pickled peppers,' said the tiny voice. 'Where's the peck of pickled peppers Peter Piper picked?'

'Huh?' said Fergal. One minute the whoever-whatever in the hole had been calling for help and now he-she-or-it was reciting tongue-twisters!

'There's no one down there, Fergal,' Mr Peach explained. 'I was having a bit of fun with you. I'm a ventriloquist.'

'*You* just said those Piper-pickling words?' gasped Fergal. 'But I didn't see your lips move.'

Mr Peach swelled with pride.

'Hardly surprising with that great big moustache

to hide them behind,' muttered a distinctly unimpressed Joshua.

Mr Peach's cheeks went peach-coloured.

'Don't be rude, Joshua!' snapped Jackie.

The twin muttered an apology.

'Say something else, Mr Peach,' urged Albie.

Mr Peach stopped in his tracks and put the luggage on the ground. He opened his valise and produced – not a ventriloquist's dummy, but a strange glove puppet of a snake, which he proceeded to slip over his left hand.

The snake then opened and closed its mouth as it appeared to recite the following poem:

I used to think the world was flat,
Not rounded like a bowler hat,
I used to think the sky was blue,
But I was told 'That's nothing new',
I used to think the sea was wet,
(That's something one should not forget),
I used to wish my poems rhymed,
And still do wish it all the time.

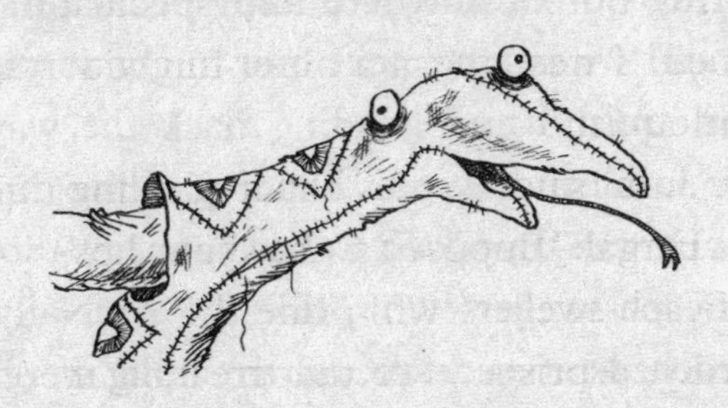

Fergal was impressed. Even though he ignored the puppet and looked directly at Mr Peach, there was nothing to suggest that the man was really doing the talking. It wasn't just that his lips weren't moving. His Adam's apple in his neck wasn't moving either and there was nothing in his expression to suggest that he was trying to look as if he *wasn't* talking, if you see what I mean. He really seemed to be watching the snake and listening to the poem too.

Moustache or no moustache, there was no denying that Mr Peach was a good ventriloquist. He pulled the snake glove puppet off his hand, stuffed it back into his valise and picked up the luggage. 'Come on!' he said. 'If you want to get to the city, we'd better get moving and try to get that lift.'

Fortunately for the passengers off the coach, quite a crowd had formed the other side of the hole. Those cars not occupied by people wanting to stand and gawp at the hole, marvelling at it, appearing out of nowhere and speculating as to when and where the next one might form, were turning around and heading back the way they came . . . in other words, heading in the direction the coach was supposed to have gone.

Many passengers who, like the McNallys and Mr Peach, ventured around the hole, were given lifts in next to no time. (The grey-haired matron-of-honour-to-be was one of the first.) Because Jackie insisted that she, Albie, Joshua and Fergal (still dressed as an enormous baby) all travelled together, people were unwilling to take them. The obvious excuse was 'no room' but, to be fair, a bunch of freckle-faced McNallys in their strange clothes might not be every driver's first choice of hitch-hiker, even if s/he was driving an empty minibus.

'It's been very kind of you to wait with us, Mr Peach,' said Jackie after yet another driver had refused them a lift, 'but I think you'd be far more likely to get into town on your own.'

'But I hate to leave you like this,' said Mr Peach.

'We quite understand,' said Jackie.

'We can look after ourselves, can't we, Albie?' said Albie, pretending to be Joshua.

'Of course we can, Joshua,' said Joshua, pretending to be Albie.

'Well, if you're sure . . .' said Mr Peach, hesitantly. 'But if you need help once you're in the city, look me up.' He pulled his calling card out of his top pocket. 'Call me if you need me, though I have a feeling we'll be meeting again anyhow!'

'Thank you,' said Jackie, putting the card away carefully.

Not five minutes later the ventriloquist got a lift

from a family who'd been planning a trip to an aunt in the country but had now decided to turn around and head for home.

Eventually, Jackie, Joshua, Albie and Fergal did get a lift, not in the back of a truck full of pigs and straw, as usually happens in such stories, but in the cab of a breakdown truck. The driver was a very jolly man called Noble and he was glad of the company. There was one big bench seat, running the width of the cab, and they all squeezed in next to each other, with their luggage fitted in around them.

Noble, whom the McNallys all later agreed looked rather like a giant vegetable – a turnip or a swede – but with hair sprouting out everywhere, was not only Noble by name but noble by nature. When he found out where they wanted to go, he drove them all the way to the back of The Dell hotel. He would have driven them right up to the entrance, of course, but Jackie had specifically asked him not to do that.

On the journey to the city, Noble had them singing car songs. You know the kind: *Ten Green Bottles*, *Row, Row, Row Your Boat*, *Old McDonald Had a Farm* and one the McNallys hadn't heard before called *I'll Tickle Thomas*. When it was your turn to sing, you had to think up a new place to tickle Thomas, and then, in the chorus, everyone had to remember – in the correct order – where Thomas had already been tickled. For those of you who hate sing-along-join-in songs, that journey in the breakdown truck would have been a living hell; but Noble and the McNallys had a great time. The twins, of course, wanted to tickle Thomas in rude places but knew that Jackie wouldn't let them, so did a lot of whispering of suggestions and giggling between them. Fergal wanted to tickle Thomas not 'under the chin' or 'on the nose' but 'under the bridge' or 'on the way home', which Noble thought was very clever!

Fergal loved being in the cab looking out at the road in front of them. The windscreen was covered in squashed flies and bugs and could have done with a very good clean, but Fergal didn't care. This was great . . . and he didn't have to pretend to be a baby, for fear of being thrown off. If the truth be told, he was glad that stupid hole had opened up in front of the coach. This was much more fun.

Although they'd lost time on the journey with the coach having broken down and their having to wait so long for a lift, Noble drove his battered breakdown truck much faster than any coach could go, so Jackie and the others weren't that late for their rendezvous with Le Fay. But late is late, and Le Fay was nowhere to be seen.

Noble drove off with a cheery wave from the cab of his truck, but didn't honk his horn. He probably guessed that Jackie and the others planned to stay at the hotel without necessarily telling the management or actually . . . er . . . paying!

*

Whilst the rest of the family were singing *I'll Tickle Thomas* with Noble, Le Fay McNally was putting her plan into action. She'd met the other finalists at the 'Meet the Other Finalists' finger buffet in the Bellhop Suite at one o'clock and, an hour later, she'd met the press at the 'Meet the Press', being 'A Photo Call with some of the Capital City's Leading Evening Newspapers'.

The finger buffet had been a relief to Le Fay. There hadn't been a finger to eat in sight, but nor was there a knife, fork or spoon, so she deduced what a finger buffet must be: a buffet where you didn't eat fingers but ate *with* your fingers! All the food was pretty much bite-size. It tasted good, but she was really glad that she'd eaten that chicken sandwich and drunk that hot chocolate up in her room. That'd been the best sandwich – and the best chicken – Le Fay had ever tasted. (Apologies to any vegetarian readers for going on about it.)

Le Fay now got to meet the two other finalists she hadn't already met, and liked them. Graham 'Lard' Large, whose dad owned Large Lunches, kept his distance, glaring at her whenever their eyes met by chance. Peggy Snoot was very polite and said 'How-do-you-do?' and shook Le Fay's hand. She asked her where she lived and whether she'd had a nice journey. When Le Fay got all excited about the train and the taxi ride, Peggy listened politely and didn't say anything boastful or nasty when Le Fay explained she'd never been on a train or in a taxi before.

Anna Malting explained that she'd been in the toughest heats to get this far in the competition so, by rights, she should have won already . . . but Le Fay could see that she was really nervous underneath and, by the end of the buffet, they were chatting together happily about animals. Anna had three gerbils, two hamsters and a guinea pig, but wasn't allowed a cat. Le Fay told her about Smoky, but didn't mention that he wasn't a pet but a rat-catcher, because she imagined gerbils, hamsters and guinea pigs were probably a bit like rats, so it might upset her.

'Why's he called Smoky?' asked Anna.

'Mum gave him that name,' said Le Fay. 'She named all of us.'

'I wish I had a cat,' said Anna, and the two girls found they'd become firm friends.

The 'Photo Call with some of the Capital City's Leading Evening Newspapers' wasn't quite what Le Fay had expected. She wasn't sure *what* she'd expected, but it wasn't three very young and bored-looking men in crumpled suits. Two had cameras with flash bulbs. The third had a notepad and a pen.

Malcolm from Tap 'n' Type made a short speech, as though talking to a room full of people, with the four finalists lined up behind him. The photographers took plenty of photos, and the man with the notepad sucked the end of his pen and didn't write anything down.

When the 'photo call' was finished, Malcolm passed a piece of paper headed PRESS RELEASE to him. The man muttered his thanks and stuffed it in a pocket of his jacket.

Just then, the door burst open and in came a man wearing an electric-blue suit, with a gleaming chrome camera around his neck.

'I'm sorry I'm late!' he said, sounding flustered.

'That's fine,' said Malcolm, stepping forward. 'Which paper are you from?'

'*Large Lunch Latest*,' said the man in the blue suit, walking straight past him.

'I . . . er . . .' Malcolm had obviously never heard of it.

'It's a newspaper for people who work in my father's company,' said Graham Large, stepping forward grandly. 'My father thought his workers would like to see a picture of me on the front page of the next issue.' He then turned his attention to the photographer. 'I was beginning to think you weren't coming!' he snapped.

'S-Sorry, Master Large,' said the man. He proceeded to take a series of stomach-churning pictures of Graham Large preening himself like a peacock. I expect that if the poor employees of Large Lunches ever saw the final full-colour photo on the front of their company newspaper, it put them off work for the rest of the day.

Le Fay didn't hang around to watch the one-boy photo session. This was the part of the itinerary where she had 'A Free Afternoon for Sightseeing'. In other words, she needed to go and wedge open the fire door at the side of the hotel, then meet Jackie, Fergal, Albie and Joshua around the back.

She took the lift back up to her room and took a box of tissues from the en suite bathroom. This would be thick enough to keep the door open, and thin enough not to make it too obvious. Making her way back down the now familiar route of the drab fire-exit stairs, her tummy had never felt so full in her life. She couldn't wait to get the rest of the family – except for grumpy old Captain Rufus, of course – up to her room to order them chicken sandwiches and chocolate.

At the foot of the stairs at last, Le Fay pushed the bar to the fire-exit door and swung it open a fraction, ready to wedge the box of tissues in place. There was a loud ringing in her ears.

She'd set off an alarm!

Chapter Six

Le Fay didn't panic. She slipped out into the street and began walking ever so casually along the pavement, looking as if she didn't have a care in the world. She glanced up at the clock on a building opposite. Five minutes to three. The others should be there soon, but how was she going to get them inside now? What she needed was Plan B, and she didn't have a Plan B!

The hotel alarm stopped and The Dell's chief house detective, Twinkle-Toes Tweedy picked up the squashed tissue box wedging the fire-exit door open. He looked out into the street – left and right – making a mental note of the people he saw there. He then swung the door shut. Le Fay didn't see him, of course, because she was walking away from the scene of her 'crime'.

She walked around the block a few times, keeping an eye out for her brothers and sister.

Three-fifteen came and went, and there was still no sign of them. She had no way of knowing that the coach had been abandoned and that they were, at that moment, in the cab of a breakdown truck singing *I'll Tickle Thomas*, as they reached the outskirts of the city.

When the clock across the street read 3.30, Le Fay decided to go back up to her room to call the coach company. Jackie had given her the number, 'in case of emergency', when she'd bought the tickets.

Le Fay walked through the brass and glass revolving door into the fabulous foyer of The Dell. Everything gleamed. It all looked so clean and shiny to Le Fay. Her jaw had dropped in wonder when Malcolm had led her through it a few hours earlier, and it seemed just as magical now.

She made her way across a carpet so plush that even her light weight sank into the pile. She reached up and pressed a button to call the lift. A man in a checked suit appeared, as if out of nowhere, at her side.

'Hello, little lady,' he said quietly. 'And where might you be going?'

Le Fay pulled her door key out of the pocket at the front of her dress. 'To my room,' she said, nervously. She knew she looked out of place in such a swanky hotel.

'So you're a guest, are you?' said the man.

'Yes,' said Le Fay. 'I'm a finalist in the Tap 'n' Type competition here tomorrow.'

'That's great,' said the man. 'Congratulations.'

Le Fay looked up at the man properly. He had a kind, round face. 'Are you a guest too?'

He shook his head. 'No. I'm Charlie Tweedy,' he said. 'I'm the hotel's chief house detective.'

Le Fay went bright red.

'Don't I know you from somewhere?' said Tweedy. 'Your face seems very familiar.'

'I don't think so, Mr Tweedy,' said Le Fay.

At that moment, the lift door opened. Le Fay hurried inside. Twinkle-Toes stayed in the foyer. 'Nice meeting you, Miss . . .?'

'Le Fay.'

'Miss Le Fay,' he said. 'Good luck in the competition tomorrow.'

'Th-Thanks,' stuttered Le Fay as the lift doors closed. Tweedy stared into her eyes and she could imagine him reading all her inner thoughts. She gulped. She had to smuggle Jackie, Fergal and the twins not only into the hotel, but also past Mr Tweedy. Things were getting tougher by the minute.

Twinkle-Toes Tweedy's office wasn't really an office at all – which makes this sentence an oxymoron (which may sound like an idiot with breathing difficulties, but actually means something that contradicts itself, such as the statement: 'All light is dark.'), but I'm sure you know what I'm getting at. He thought of it more as a cubbyhole but, if the truth be told, what it really was was a large built-in hotel linen cupboard with the door taken off. You could see on the door frame where the hinges had once been. The spaces had been painted over, but even the screw-holes were still there. To the left of the door frame was a sign printed on to card which read:

CAPTAIN C. TWEEDY (RETD)
CHIEF HOUSE DETECTIVE

in a typeface that Tweedy secretly thought was better suited to a menu in a swish Manhattan restaurant than announcing a man of his profession. The 'retd' in brackets meant that he was a retired captain, not a retired house detective. No, sir. He was still very much on the case when it came to odd goings-on in *his* hotel.

Under this official sign, provided by The Dell management, was an unofficial sign added in the detective's own, fine handwriting. It read:

MY DOOR IS ALWAYS OPEN

which those of you with more intelligence than a cake of soap – which, no doubt, includes *most* readers of this quality book – will realise was, at least partly, a joke . . . because his cupboard/cubbyhole/office had no door. Having said that (which is what I've just done), Twinkle-Toes Tweedy would have had an open-door policy even if he'd had a door. In other words, door or no door, his door (or no door) was always metaphorically open. Clear? Don't lie.

Let me put it another way: Captain Twinkle-Toes Tweedy (retd) didn't believe in shutting himself away and making himself self-important, unlike a number of ex-policemen who ended up in private security jobs. Twinkle-Toes thought that the best way to keep law and order in a big hotel like The Dell was to know all the latest gossip and rumour, and the best way to do that was to welcome anyone and everyone who felt like coming to his office for a nice chat and a cup of something hot.

When junior management came in for a chat, they'd describe it as 'touching base' or 'keeping him informed'. If one of the women from the laundry came in, she might say that it was for a 'good old chin-wag'. Golgotha (the man who looked after the boiler and central heating) called it 'a jaw' and the ladies from the waitress staff might have 'a good old natter'. Other expressions for talking to Twinkle-Toes included 'a chit-chat', 'sharing the craik' (pronounced 'crack') and, more honestly than most, 'having a good old gossip' or 'dishing the dirt'.

In order to make sure that people kept on coming back to him, the house detective had three important rules:

1. Never to reveal his sources.
2. Always to have a good supply of tea and coffee.
3. Always to have a good supply of the very best chocolate biscuits in the hotel.

Number one was so that people wouldn't be afraid to tell him things. If a bit of gossip led to him catching members of staff stealing, for example, he'd never let slip who might have pointed him in their direction.

Number two was straightforward enough, except that at the time that these events took place, as well as huge holes springing up out of nowhere, there was a terrible world coffee shortage, for some reason. Don't ask me why. It probably had something to do with a severe frost in the main coffee-growing countries killing off all the little coffee beans, but I'm only guessing. Although I'm married to someone called Doctor Coffey – it's true, I promise you (her name is spelled with an 'ey' instead of an 'ee') – that doesn't make her a coffee expert either. Anyway, getting hold of a catering pack of 1,000 teabags was no problem for old Twinkle-Toes, but having so much as a small jar of instant coffee to hand meant that the retired police detective had to call in a lot of old favours, twist a lot of arms and pull a few strings (to involve as many metaphors as possible). Whilst many of the guests were being served poor quality coffee mixed with chicory, down in Twinkle-Toes Tweedy's office you could actually get yourself a cup of the stuff that actually tasted like coffee!

The chocolate biscuits were the icing on the cake, if you see what I mean. They were to bait those who weren't hooked by the 'never-reveal-his-sources' or 'chance-of-a-decent-cuppa' rules.

Sitting in Tweedy's cubbyhole that afternoon,

sipping a cup of the detective's prized coffee, was Mrs Doon, head of housekeeping. It was her team of women whose job it was to make the beds and clean the rooms in The Dell. It was also their job to replace the boxes of tissues when they were empty.

On the desk between them sat the crumpled box of tissues that Le Fay McNally had used to wedge the fire door open, and triggered off the alarm in so doing.

'It's definitely from one of the rooms, is it not, Mrs Doon?' the detective was asking.

'Either that, or taken from the stock room or from one of my girls' cleaning carts, Mr T,' replied Mrs Doon. She always referred to Captain Tweedy as 'Mr T' and her team of chambermaids as 'her girls'. Some of them were girls, barely of school-leaving age. Some of them were not. Some of them had grandchildren or even great-grandchildren. To call them 'girls' was a bit like calling the pope 'slightly religious'. It was misleading, to say the least. The cleaning carts she also mentioned, by the way, were the carts 'her girls' left outside the rooms as they cleaned, containing replacement bars of soap, sachets of shampoo and shower gel and little boxes of neatly furled shower caps. (I'm not 100 per cent sure one can furl, or unfurl, a shower cap but, as one can furl and unfurl a flag, I thought why not give it a go.)

'Good point,' said Twinkle-Toes Tweedy. 'And your girls are unlikely to be able to tell if someone took a packet off their carts, aren't they?'

'I'm afraid so,' said Mrs Doon.

'Do many guests take the tissues with them when they leave?' asked Tweedy.

He knew the answer before he asked it. He'd worked there long enough. He knew that the average guest took all the toiletries in the bathroom; then there were those who stole the bath plug along with the odd towel or three as well; and then there were those who took all of that, plus the tissues, plus just about anything else that wasn't nailed down or that could be smuggled out. Some chancers even lowered the television sets out of their windows to accomplices waiting below. Once Tweedy had caught a man trying to leave the hotel with an ironing board and a full-length mirror (which he'd unscrewed from the inside of the wardrobe door) inside a zip-up cover designed to contain a surfboard, carried out along with a whole host of other sporting gear from skis to lacrosse rackets! It turned out that the thief had been stealing ironing boards and full-length mirrors in all the hotels around town and no one had been able to work out how, so Tweedy was a local hero among hotel house detectives for a while.

'Yes, a number of them take the tissues, as you well know, Mr T,' said Mrs Doon. 'But the majority leave them be.'

'Well, what I'd like you to do is to instruct your girls to let you know which rooms on the east side of the building are without boxes of tissues tomorrow morning, please, Mrs Doon. I'd be extremely grateful.' He'd said 'east side' because the tissue box had been wedged in the door of one of the east-side fire exits. Of course, the door-wedger might have deliberately come all the way from the north, south or west side to be as far from their room as possible, but Tweedy needed to narrow the search somehow. And, anyway, he had a hunch.

'Of course, Mr T,' said The Dell's housekeeper. 'Anything you say . . . Any chance of another chocky bickie and another cup of coffee?'

Captain Twinkle-Toes Tweedy spooned out the coffee granules into a fresh cup as though they were gold dust. '*Of course*, Launa,' he grinned.

Le Fay wondered what to do next. She decided that all she *could* do was go back downstairs and hang around outside the hotel, trying to keep as inconspicuous as possible, until her family showed up. She closed her door, hurried across the landing to the lift and pressed the button, imagining the large house detective watching her every move. The man had been very polite and everything, but that was probably one of the tricks of the trade, to keep criminals off their guard so that they'd slip up and make a mistake. Not that she was a real criminal, of course, but she was planning to get five of them sleeping in a room meant for one!

There was a 'ping' and the lift doors opened. Le Fay's greatest fear was that she'd find Tweedy already inside, or the dreadful Graham Large. To her relief, there were a handful of total strangers. She smiled at them. One or two smiled back and the rest of them looked straight ahead (as people in lifts so often do) and she stepped inside.

The lift stopped on five more floors on the way down and, fortunately for Le Fay, no one familiar entered. Once in the foyer, she strode purposefully out of the entrance and took up position on the other side of the street.

She didn't have to wait long. Once Jackie and the others had been dropped off at the side of the hotel by that nice Mr Noble, Jackie had decided that they should walk briskly around the block until Le Fay put in an appearance . . . and, sure enough, here they were now.

Albie caught sight of Le Fay before she saw them. He nudged his twin, Joshua, in the ribs. 'There she is!' he said.

''Bout time too,' said Josh, who was feeling hungry.

They ran across to reach Le Fay, who, rather than stopping and hugging them, started walking off. 'Keep moving,' she instructed.

It was only when they were around the corner from the entrance and the possible prying eyes of the doorman, that Le Fay gave each of them a hug and a kiss.

'You made it!' she said.

'What's the hotel like?' asked Fergal excitedly. 'Does your room have a bath or a shower? Does it have feather pillows?'

'Is there a television?' asked Albie.

'Are there blankets or a duvet?' asked Joshua.

'Do they feed you?' asked Fergal.

'Give the girl a chance!' laughed Jackie, in her big-sister role.

'What kept you?' asked Le Fay.

'Holes!' the twins chorused as one.

'A great big one opened up in front of the coach,' Fergal explained. 'We got a lift from a man in a pick-up truck.'

'Save that story for later,' said Jackie. 'Have you found a way to get us inside?' she asked Le Fay.

'I had a brilliant plan,' said Le Fay, and she told them about the back stairs, the fire exit and setting off the alarm.

'Oh dear,' said Jackie. 'I'm beginning to think you'll never be able to smuggle us in there!'

Chapter Seven

In the end, after all that planning and worrying, getting her sister and brothers into the hotel and up to her room was as easy as pie. Why pie should be easy I've never been quite sure. I personally have trouble making pastry, so would rather say 'as easy as stew', but the saying is 'as easy as pie', so I feel safer sticking with that.

Le Fay, Jackie, Albie, Joshua and Fergal were all standing around the corner from the entrance to The Dell, trying to come up with a Plan B, when Malcolm Kent from Tap 'n' Type appeared, shopping bag in hand.

'Hello, Le Fay,' he said. 'How are you enjoying things so far?'

'Very much, thank you,' said Le Fay.

Malcolm put down his bag of shopping. 'This must be your family,' he said (which, with their wiry ginger-red hair, freckles and – with the exception of Jackie – buck teeth, was an easy assumption to make). He put out his hand and shook Jackie's. 'Aren't you going to introduce me?'

'She's my big sister, Jackie,' said Le Fay.

'How do you do?' said Malcolm.

'How do you do?' said Jackie.

Back then, that was the correct response to a how-do-you-do? Nowadays people respond with a 'fine, thanks; how about you?' and then the first person says 'fine', and it takes up far too much time.

'Here to support Le Fay at the competition? Lovely.'

'I'm Albie,' said Joshua.

'And I'm Josh,' said Albie.

'I rather suspect it's the other way around,' said Malcolm as he shook their hands, which was pretty impressive, since he'd never even met them before.

'How on Earth did you know that?' asked Le Fay, so impressed that she forgot her shyness.

'Well, if I was a young near-identical twin, I think I'd pretend to be the other one, just to confuse grown-ups,' said Malcolm. 'And last but not least?'

'I'm Fergal,' said Fergal. 'The brains of the family!' which, as time will show, was rather an ironic thing to say.

'A pleasure to meet you too,' said Malcolm. 'Are you staying locally?'

'At a B&B,' said Jackie hurriedly. The tip of her nose went pink, which the McNallys knew meant that she was telling a fib.

Malcolm picked up his shopping bag and turned to Le Fay. 'Why not show them your room before they check into their B&B?' he suggested. 'That way they can see you're all settled in and ready for tomorrow's competition.'

Fergal had no idea what a 'B&B' was and was still impressed by Jackie's quick thinking . . . and delighted that they'd found a way inside. Of course, the poor chap had no way of knowing that this would be the building he'd fall to his death from; but perhaps that was a good thing. Think how gloomy *that* piece of news would have made him.

It turned out that Malcolm had nipped out to buy some additional balloons and streamers to add the finishing touches to the room where the grand finals of the competition were to take place. He was showing Jackie the contents of his shopping bag as they sauntered through the entrance of The Dell and walked over to the row of lift doors. Being with Malcolm of Tap 'n' Type and Le Fay, who was booked in with a room, the others felt as though they had every right to be there, so didn't look in the least bit shifty. Shabby?

Yes. Shifty? No. Not that they had any intention of looking around their sister's room and then heading off to check into some non-existent bed-and-breakfast place.

Once Le Fay had proudly fished the golden key out of her pocket and unlocked the door, the others piled into her hotel room and went over every inch of it.

They all liked the en suite bathroom best. You turned on the taps and water came straight out – *hot* water at that, if that's what you wanted – and there was a shower *and* a bath . . . and it was all just for them. Well, just for Le Fay really, but the five of them would be using it (sooner rather than later, as it turned out).

In fact, the first thing Jackie insisted on was that they each had a bath or a shower, one after the other. Now, one or two of you may not be a big fan of washing, but the good thing is, if you *have* to wash – say you've fallen on a doggy doo or something – it's good to know that there's hot water if you need it. For the McNallys, a shower was when it wasn't raining very hard and a bath was a very rare event in an old tin tub, so they had a great time washing.

By the end of it, their skins had never looked so pink and they'd never felt – and smelled – so clean!

Le Fay told them about the chicken sandwich and the mug of hot chocolate you could get by picking up the phone and just asking.

'I could do that just before I go off to supper,' said Le Fay, checking her itinerary ('Dinner with our Generous Sponsors in the Sizzle Grill at eight o'clock').

'But they'll be rather suspicious if you ask for four more sandwiches and four more cups of hot chocolate,' said Fergal. 'We don't want to risk being found out.'

'Good point,' said Le Fay, thinking back to her brief encounter with Captain Charlie 'Twinkle-Toes' Tweedy, chief house detective.

'I don't think it's only chicken sandwiches you have to order,' said Jackie, who was that much older so, though never having been to a hotel before either, knew that much more about room service. 'If you ordered a large piece of fish with extra chips, that should easily feed the four of us, and they'll simply assume that you're really, really hungry. Try asking for cod.'

'OK,' said Le Fay, doubtfully. She picked up the phone and dialled '1'. When the woman answered at the other end, Le Fay asked for a large piece of cod with extra chips.

'Breaded or battered?' asked the voice.

Le Fay had no idea that 'breaded' meant covered in breadcrumbs, so said, 'Battered please,' (which you might have guessed, if you remembered what I said on page 11).

'One large battered cod and chips with extra chips,' said the woman. 'It comes with a selection of sauces: vinegar, brown sauce, ketchup. Would you like anything to drink?'

Le Fay put her hand over the receiver. 'Drink?' she asked.

Jackie shook her head. 'We'll have water from the tap,' she whispered.

Le Fay spoke into the telephone. 'No thank you,' she said.

'It'll be with you in half an hour, dear,' said the woman from Room Service. 'Room 1428.'

Fergal, Joshua, Albie and Jackie hid in the bathroom when the knock on the door came and the food was delivered. The waiter'd barely gone when they piled back into the bedroom and inspected the food he'd left on the tray.

'It's a feast!' said Joshua excitedly, grabbing a

chip. Jackie slapped the back of his hand. 'That's one less chip for you. We share this out equally.'

The other three groaned, but they knew that fair was fair and that, if anyone had a little less than the others, it'd be Jackie herself. Her excuse was that she had less growing to do.

Le Fay looked on, proud that, whether she won or not, her getting this far in the competition had got them all a night in a hotel room away from their father, which, in turn, had got them a good meal and plenty of baths!

When Le Fay went downstairs for her supper, Jackie made the others sit on the bed and watch television with the sound down low, because they didn't want to arouse suspicion. (She'd made them wash their greasy fingers first, though.)

Fergal was so excited to get his hands on the remote control that he kept on wanting to change channels all the time. Jackie made them start off by watching a nature documentary on grizzly bears. Soon they were all watching it, open-mouthed. The picture was so clear it was almost as if they were there in the mountains with the bears.

'I wish we could stay in this hotel room for ever,' said Albie.

'Me too,' sighed Jackie.

*

The next morning was the morning of the Grand Final of the Tap 'n' Type competition. Although Le Fay had slept in the bed because, after all, it was her typing skill that had got them the room in the first place, she'd had a pretty sleepless night. She'd been lying awake thinking of nasty Graham Large with his spun-sugar hair, and the fear of losing to him of all people. Albie had slept on the sofa and Joshua had slept on the sofa cushions on the floor. Fergal had slept in the open bottom drawer of the chest of drawers (with extra pillows, found in the top of the closet, for padding). Jackie had slept under a blanket in the bath, when she wasn't on the prowl.

Le Fay had come back from the previous night's meal with a 'doggy bag'. Malcolm had spotted her slipping a bread roll into the pocket of her dress and asked one of the waiters to bring him a paper bag.

'If there's anything you can't finish now but

might want to eat later, pop it in here,' he had told the appreciative girl. 'Everyone does it!' he'd said. Malcolm, who started out a nice chap in this story was beginning to turn into a very nice one. If the truth be told, Le Fay hadn't spotted a single other doggy bag all evening!

By the time Le Fay had made it back up to her room, the bag had been fit to burst. Whilst she now went down to breakfast with Malcolm and the other contestants, she left Jackie to share out the contents of the doggy bag for a breakfast feast.

When Le Fay entered the Sun Deck Breakfast Restaurant, Peggy Snoot and Anna Malting were already seated at a round table covered with a cream-coloured linen tablecloth. Peggy was polite as always, and Anna was eager to talk about all the different fruits and cereals and how much her gerbils would have liked eating them for their breakfast. (Le Fay wondered if Smoky had caught any rats while they were away.)

Malcolm wandered over to the table with a fruit juice in his hand. He'd been getting a refill. 'Good morning, Le Fay,' he smiled. 'Sleep well?'

'The bed was very comfortable but I was awake thinking about the competition for a lot of the time,' confessed Le Fay.

'Me too,' said Anna, 'I was so excited.'

'And I'm so nervous,' said Peggy.

'So am I,' said Malcolm, 'and I'm not even taking part.'

The girls were laughing at this as the shadow of Graham Large's quiff appeared over the mini-pots of marmalade and jam in the centre of the table.

'Good morning,' he said. 'I was hoping for a separate table.'

'We need to sit together so that I can fill you all in on the day's events,' said Malcolm. 'Sorry.'

The boy sat in the seat between Le Fay and Malcolm. She could smell his scented, oiled skin and the various gels and sprays in his hair. It was a bit like walking past the perfume counter in a department store, with all the competing smells mingling into one very expensive one.

No wonder he's the last one down to breakfast, thought Le Fay. He must take hours preparing himself.

'How did you sleep?' Malcolm asked the boy.

'Terribly,' said Graham Large. 'There was a drip coming from my shower and the noise kept me awake . . .'

'Couldn't you have shut the bathroom door?' Peggy suggested. 'Surely that would have blocked out the noise?'

'But I would have known that it was still dripping,' said Graham, 'which would have been just as bad.'

'I'm sorry to hear that,' said Malcolm, though he later revealed that he wasn't sorry at all. Graham Large had a whole suite of rooms and if the drip-drip-drip had bothered his poor little sensitive soul that much, he could have slept on the pull-out bed in the sitting room, far far away from the bathroom.

'So what did you do?' asked Anna.

'I called the night porter and had him fix it.'

'Wow!' said Anna, clearly impressed. 'What time was that?'

'About three o'clock in the morning.'

'I'll bet he loved you,' Le Fay muttered under her breath. She and Graham had avoided eye contact since he'd sat down.

Graham pretended not to have heard her. 'It's what these people are here for, of course,' he said. 'To serve.' He snapped his podgy fingers together and cried out, '*Garçon*,' which Le Fay knew from her French lessons meant 'boy'.

A waiter in a red waistcoat appeared by their table. 'Sir?' he said, raising an eyebrow.

'Four on a raft and wreck 'em,' he said. 'White bread, and weak tea. China. And I mean weak.'

'Sir,' nodded the waiter. He seemed to understand what Graham Large had wanted, even though it'd sounded to Le Fay as if he'd been talking in code. (The 'four' referred to in 'four on a raft and wreck 'em' meant four eggs; the 'raft' was the toast on which they'd be served, which Graham had specified should be made from white bread. The 'wreck 'em' referred to the fact that the eggs should be scrambled.)

'Would anyone else like to order?' asked the waiter, turning to the others with a much more human expression.

'Ladies?' said Malcolm. 'You can have bacon, fried egg, poached egg, boiled egg, scrambled egg, sausage, beans, mushrooms, kippers, waffles . . . You name it, they've got it.' He turned to Le Fay. 'Of course, that's after you've helped yourself to fruit, fruit juices and cereals from the table over there.'

Le Fay felt as if she'd gone to Heaven. Little did

she realise that, less than twelve hours later, that's where everyone would be telling her Fergal had gone, to try to make her feel better after the SPLAT! incident. She settled for bacon, sausage, mushroom, beans and a fried egg. For those of you interested in food, Anna stuck with cereal and toast and Anna had a plate of waffles and maple syrup. Malcolm had three kippers.

Le Fay had just cut into her sausage when Graham spoke. 'I know they'd be called stowaways if we were on board ship,' he said, 'but what do you call people who hide away in other people's hotel rooms without paying? Apart from "thieves", that is?' Le Fay stopped cutting and stared at her plate.

'What is this?' asked Malcolm. 'A crossword clue?'

'No, it is a matter of grave concern,' said Master Large.

'What do you mean?' asked Malcolm.

'I mean that I believe there to be people staying in this hotel who are here without the management's knowledge or permission,' said Graham.

Malcolm fixed the boy's eyes in a stare. 'I understood that perfectly,' he said, 'but what I don't understand is why that should be of grave concern to you. Unless Large Lunches has part ownership in this hotel?'

'No,' said Graham, a little put out, 'but don't you think it any honest citizen's duty to report a crime if he discovers one?'

'Absolutely,' agreed Malcolm, pulling a tiny fishbone from between his teeth. 'So where are these hotel-equivalent of stowaways? Hiding in the boiler room? Living behind the pot plants in the Palm Court Tea Room?'

Peggy giggled. Graham Large gave her the benefit of one of his nasty sneers. Le Fay kept on staring at her plate.

'I happened to get out of the lift on the wrong floor on my way down to breakfast,' said Large, turning to look directly at Le Fay now. 'I was walking past Room 1428, which, I would imagine from the closeness of the doors to each other was a single room' – he said the word 'single' as though it was something very nasty he'd just trodden in – 'when I heard a whole gaggle of whispering voices.'

'And what leads you to believe that these guests are – how shall I put it? – "uninvited"?' asked Malcolm. He knew full well that Le Fay's room number was 1428. Of course he did. He'd shown Le Fay to it only the day before. He also knew full well that Graham Large knew full well that it was Le Fay's room and, although Malcolm had no idea about the boy's visit to her room or the Large/Lard incident, he didn't like what Graham was up to (whatever the reason).

'Because I heard one of them say, "Keep the noise down, you don't want anyone to hear us."'

That would have been sensible Jackie, keeping order as always, thought Le Fay.

Malcolm put his knife and fork together on his plate and pushed it away from him. 'You're not quite the detective you think you are, Graham,' said Malcolm. 'The room you just mentioned is Le Fay's and, if you'd been up as early as she and I were, you'd have known that her family turned up first thing this morning ready to cheer her along at the competition. With all the hotel reception rooms so quiet this time of the morning, I suggested that they go up to Le Fay's room while we had breakfast. As for wanting to 'keep the noise down', the McNallys seem a very considerate family and wouldn't dream of interrupting the other guests . . . Think how much that dripping tap upset you!'

Le Fay couldn't believe what she was hearing. She wanted to throw her arms around Malcolm from Tap 'n' Type and give him a great big HUG! He must have realised that the whole 'B&B' business was made up and that the others had been there all night, but he was lying through his teeth for her.

Somewhat deflated, Graham Large suddenly looked a little smaller. Le Fay tucked into the remains of her breakfast with relish.

Chapter Eight

The Tap 'n' Type grand finals were introduced by the Chairman of Tap 'n' Type, Count Medoc Silverman. Count Medoc wore a pinstripe suit, but the stripes must have been drawn with a pretty thick pin because they were pretty thick stripes. He stood to the front of the stage in The Dell's Empress Conference Suite and explained to the audience how the competition would proceed.

'Above my head are four giant screens,' he said, though you'd have had to have your eyes shut or been blind to miss them. 'And each screen is connected to the keyboard of an individual finalist. That way we'll be able to see each and every letter appear as they type.'

There was a ripple of applause, mainly from Tap 'n' Type employees, who thought it was safer to clap at everything their chairman said, just in case he was offended if they didn't.

Each screen was labelled with a contestant's name. Top left read: G. LARGE; bottom left: P. SNOOT; top right: A. MALTING; and bottom right: L. MCNALLY.

There'd been some discussion between the organisers as to whether it should have been 'LF. MCNALLY', her first name being Le Fay, but it was decided that it was fairer if they were all given just one initial each.

Count Silverman went on to explain that it was a knock-out competition. At the end of each round of typing, the contestant with the lowest score would drop out of the competition. This meant that the final round would be a head-to-head between the two best typists . . . but there'd be only one winner.

On the word 'winner', the audience applauded the chairman once again. Now it was Malcolm's turn to speak. 'The first round is dictation,' he announced. 'So that no single contestant can have the slightest advantage of being familiar with the piece read out to them, or of having, accidentally or otherwise' – his eyes came to rest on Graham Large – 'seen it written down beforehand, our four grand finalists will be typing the words of our special guest, who will be making them up as he goes along.' Malcolm paused to catch his breath. 'So let's give a big Tap 'n' Type welcome to ventriloquist and beat poet Hieronymus Peach!'

Mr Peach – yes, *that* Mr Peach: the one with the great big moustache – bounded on to the stage with his valise in his hand. He saw the McNallys in the second row (behind the Large family and friends, who'd taken up the whole front row, on each side of the central aisle) and gave them a special wink.

'He didn't tell us he'd be here!' Fergal whispered loudly to Jackie.

'Shh!' said Jackie. 'He said we'd meet again.'

'Now the rules are simple,' said Malcolm. 'In this first round, Hieronymus Peach will make up three poems on subjects chosen by the audience. The contestants will type as he speaks.' He turned to the four contestants, seated at four separate desks, with four separate keyboards and screens. 'Are you ready, Tap 'n' Type grand finalists?'

'Ready!' they said together (as rehearsed beforehand). Graham Large added a sneer and a thumbs-up to his supporters.

'Good luck, each and every one of you. May the best typist win!'

There were cheers and claps, this time more from the finalists' families and friends than from the Tap 'n' Type employees. Malcolm wasn't the chairman, so they didn't need to suck up to him.

'Come on, my boy!' boomed a voice from the front row. No prizes for guessing who that must have been. The only boy in the competition was Graham Large, so that must have been his father, Mr David Large of Large Lunches.

Jackie looked over to him. He looked like an even fatter, more perfumed and coiffured version of the boy on the stage, whom Le Fay had told her so much about. ('Coiffured' means his hair had been made to look *really lovely*.)

'So let's choose a topic for the first poem. Any suggestions?' Malcolm asked the audience.

'Holes!' shouted Fergal.

'The Moon!' shouted Jackie.

'Prize roses!' shouted a smartly dressed woman in tweeds, who later turned out to be Peggy Snoot's mum.

'Doggies!' shouted a little boy, sitting on his own near the back.

'Doggies,' said Malcolm, with a little nod. He turned to Mr Peach, who was already rummaging in his valise and pulling out a glove puppet in the shape of a black Scottie dog. 'Mr Peach, please make up your poem. Contestants, please type as he speaks . . .'

Suddenly, the dog appeared to be singing:

Don't let your doggy do
Doggy doos [full stop]
Don't let your doggy do
Doggy doos [full stop]
For if he does doggy doos [comma]
Then he'll end up
In the news [full stop]
So don't let your doggy do
Doggy doos [exclamation mark]

The Scottie dog glove puppet bowed, the audience cheered and everyone had their eyes fixed on the screens.

'Full marks to all contestants!' Malcolm announced, as Mr Peach put the puppet back in his valise.

'This isn't going to be as boring as I thought,' said Albie, who was really hoping that his sister would win and had been really looking forward to the coach journey and coming to the capital. It was just the typing part he hadn't been so thrilled about . . . and who could really blame him?

The next topic chosen by Malcolm from suggestions from the audience was 'nightmares'.

Mr Peach produced a glove puppet that looked like a gargoyle – a hideous head carved in stone. When the head began to speak, it somehow sounded old and evil and Fergal found it hard to believe that it was really the same Mr Peach who'd just made the Scottie dog appear to speak, and the snake appear to talk on the previous day.

At night when half the world is sleeping
[comma]
Into your dreams this thing comes creeping
[full stop]
Inside your head its thoughts invade
With flashes of fear from its slashing blade
[exclamation mark]
The nightmare seeps into your mind
And leaves no pretty thoughts behind
[full stop]
If you can't escape its deadly grasp
[comma]
This gasp of air – the gargoyle puppet appeared to make a desperate attempt to gulp down air – *could be your last* [full stop]

With that, the hideous head fell from the ventriloquist's hand and lay on the bare boards of the stage, still panting for breath. Those in the audience who'd spotted this leant forward with a gasp, then broke into loud cheers. This Hieronymus Peach was a crowd-pleaser.

In that poem, Anna Malting had put an apostrophe in 'its' and had left out the 'h' in 'behind' because she'd been typing too quickly. Peggy Snooting had spelled 'seeps' with an 'a'. With two poems to go in this first round, Graham Large and Le Fay McNally hadn't made a single mistake.

*

For those of you who enjoy the gruesome gory bits, thank you for your patience. You're probably far more interested in what happened to Fergal's lifeless body when the ambulance completed its journey than you are in the typing competition. Now, I could say, 'Tough luck,' but jumping forwards again has advantages for all you readers. If we can get a little more of the nasty stuff out of the way *now*, then we don't have to save it all up until the end.

Doing it this way, we've already had Fergal fall out of the window and we've already had him land on the pavement (or sidewalk, or whatever you want to call it) and we've already had him declared dead by the medical examiner and picked up by the ambulance. If we could just get his body to the morgue, then we could get back to some of the nicer, jolly stuff with him still alive.

This way, when you reach page 133, you won't

go away feeling really, really depressed but will have got used to the idea that poor little Fergal McNally is as squashed as a bug underfoot. So, to the morgue:

The ambulance pulled up at the back entrance of the Sacred Heart Hospital and backed straight up to the doors leading down to the morgue. Morris (the paramedic) jumped down and opened the rear door of his vehicle. He slid out the stretcher bearing Fergal in the black, zipped-up body bag and laid it on a gurney (which isn't an island near Jersey but a trolley on wheels).

It had started to rain and the pitter patter of raindrops on the body bag sounded to the paramedic like someone drumming their fingers on . . . on a body bag. He hoped it wasn't coming from the inside because there was no way that this DOA (Dead On Arrival) wasn't DOA (Dead On Arrival), not after the stain he'd left on the pavement.

He banged the gurney through a pair of swing doors into the dry. Now inside an old lift, he pulled the concertina doors closed, punched a button and the contraption lurched downward, taking him and Fergal McNally's lifeless body to the bowels of the hospital.

Morris wheeled the body along a dingy, ill-lit corridor (where badly lagged pipes lined the ceiling) into the pathology lab. The pathologist was nowhere to be seen, but sitting in the corner, reading a magazine, was a scruffy-looking man wearing a white coat. It was the assistant path lab assistant.

'Hi, Morris,' said the assistant path lab assistant, glancing up from an article on 'Caring for your Cacti'.

'Hi, Dennis,' said the ambulanceman.

'What have you got for us today?' asked Dennis. He put down his magazine and wandered over to the body bag.

'A young kid fell out of a hotel window,' said Morris. 'Terrible shame.'

'Terrible,' agreed Dennis, trying to look serious rather than bored. This was only a summer job, and he usually spent his summers selling ice creams over in Gerton Park. He had been hoping to sell ice creams again that year, but his cousin Barney had pipped him to the post, so he'd had to find something else to do, which is how he came to be working in the basement of the Sacred Heart.

'Where's the Doc?' asked Morris. 'The Doc' is what they all called the pathologist, who was in charge of the morgue. As well as telling everyone else what to do (which she was very good at, by the way), it was also her job to cut people open and work out exactly what they had died of by looking at the bits . . . I don't know about you, but I'm quite keen to change the subject.

With no one else around, Morris had to make do with Dennis, the assistant path lab assistant's signature. The reason why the ambulanceman was a little reluctant to get Dennis to sign was that a path lab assistant was someone a little more important than a monkey and just about as well respected as a hospital-trained cleaner. An *assistant* path lab assistant came somewhere below a monkey – if that monkey was circus-trained – in the respect department, but he did get paid more than a regular supply of bananas.

Dennis signed the ROD (Receipt Of Deceased) form and helped Morris lift the body-in-the-bag on to a stainless steel table. That done, the ambulanceman began wheeling the now empty stretcher on the gurney back down the corridor towards the rickety old lift, and Dennis got back to reading his article on cacti (which is more than one cactus).

What we could do, in the meantime, is get back to the point in the story where the first round of the typing competition was still under way, with Fergal in the audience, still very much alive.

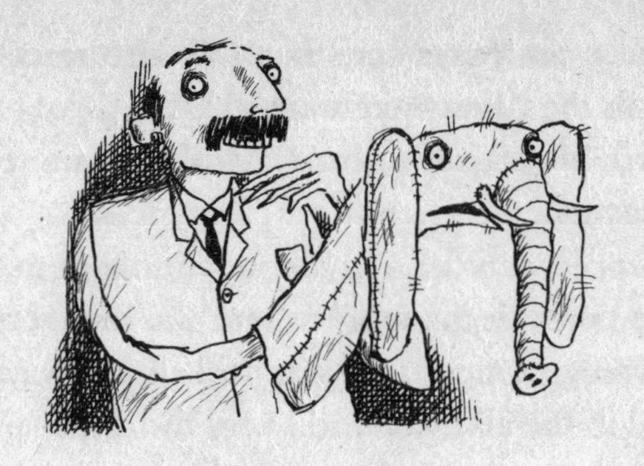

Chapter Nine

When Mr Peach had finished his fourth and final poem made up on the spot – this one was about pyramids, suggested by a grey-haired gentleman with a mop and bucket at the back – Malcolm bounded back into centre stage.

'Well, at the end of this first round, Graham Large and Le Fay McNally have yet to make a single mistake . . . Perfect scores, you two. Well done. Peggy Snoot has made two, and Anna Malting has made three . . . which means, I'm afraid, that we have to say farewell to Anna; but I must remind her that, in Tap 'n' Type's opinion, she's a winner to have reached the Grand Finals!'

He started to clap and the whole audience joined in as Anna stood up, lower lip trembling, and walked offstage. Passing Le Fay at her computer terminal, she whispered, 'I hope you win.' The two girls smiled at each other.

Anna's computer screen above the stage was switched off. Now there were three.

'In this second round,' Malcolm went on, 'Hieronymus Peach has ten sentences to say to you. Once each sentence has been spoken, you will type the words of the sentence in reverse order . . . We're not asking you to spell the words backwards, just to type the words in reverse order. For example, if he were to say, "The cat sat on the mat," you would type, "Mat the on sat cat the." Don't worry about capital letters, full stops and the like. Do worry about apostrophes. And stop typing the moment you hear the gong . . . Clear?'

'Clear!' said the three remaining contestants, who'd had it explained to them beforehand but, of course, had no idea what sentences the extraordinary Mr Peach might come up with!

'Ready, Mr Peach?'

'Ready,' said the moustached ventriloquist and beat poet. 'Sentence number one . . .' He put on the snake glove puppet the other McNallys had seen by the huge hole. 'Peter Piper picked a peck of pickled peppers.'

Le Fay frantically typed: 'peppers pickled of peck a picked piper peter,' which isn't as easy as it may sound – especially now Mr Peach already had another puppet on his hand, which appeared to be saying: 'Round and round the ragged rock the ragged rascal ran.'

'ran rascal ragged the rock rugged the round and round,' Le Fay typed.

The sentences came thick and fast (which is a phrase I've been wanting to use for ages and it seems to fit really nicely here, without a join, so long as I don't call too much attention to it).

It was in the very last sentence that Le Fay made her first mistake. What Hieronymus Peach said was: 'Are you sure she sells sea shells on the sea shore any more?'

Le Fay typed: 'more any shore sea the on shells sea sells she shore you are.' The order of the words was fine, but – in all the confusion of having to do everything backwards – she'd spelled 'sure' as 'shore'. She realised this and was just about to change it when the gong for the end of the round was sounded.

Malcolm checked the screens and totted up the scores. 'Peggy Snoot didn't make a single mistake in this round (well done, Peggy), whereas both Le Fay McNally and Graham Large made one mistake each' – Le Fay sighed with relief. She was still in the game! – 'which makes the scores at the end of this round: Graham and Le Fay with one mistake each, Peggy with two, so I'm sorry, Peggy, we have to say "Congratulations and goodbye!" to you.'

There were claps as she began to walk across the stage; then everything suddenly plunged into darkness. The clapping stopped and there were murmurs of: 'What's happening?'

'Power cut!' shouted a voice.

The reason why it was so dark without the lights was that, although there was daylight outside, all the blinds in the room had been pulled down over the windows so that the stage could be lit with electric lighting to the best effect. (It'd taken a while to eliminate any glare from the four giant computer screens above the stage – all of which had now gone blank.)

There were sounds of scurrying around and then, a minute or two later, Malcolm opened one of the blinds and sunlight streamed through a window. 'Sorry about this, folks. We'll find out what's happening and –'

At that moment, the lights came back on, the computers booted up again and three screens flickered to life. Peggy's was switched off, now that she'd left the stage, which left Graham Large's screen top left, and Le Fay McNally's bottom right.

Malcolm pulled the blind back down and jumped back up on to the stage. Out of the corner of his eye, Fergal thought he caught a flash of something electric-blue lurking in the shadows by the edge of the stage, but thought nothing of it.

'Apologies for the added drama!' said Malcolm, who'd not only proved that he was a very nice man but also that he was very good at his job. 'Now we come to the final round of the Grand Final of the Tap 'n' Type competition. By the end of this round we will be left with one runner-up and one National Champion . . .'

This final round was straightforward enough. It relied on good spelling ability and speedy typing, without errors. Mr Peach slipped on a glove puppet of a crocodile wearing a mortar board (one of those flat, square caps with a tassel on it that teachers wear in old films and graduation students throw up in the air – a bit like a carpet tile) and began a quick fire of long words: 'immediately', 'coeducation', 'disinherited', 'unnecessarily' and so on. No sooner had he finished than the gong sounded.

In their second row seats, Jackie, Albie, Joshua and Fergal had their eyes glued on Le Fay's screen and what they saw horrified them. It was full of mistakes – littered with them. You name it, she spelled it incorrectly. It was a total disaster!

Had their sister finally lost her nerve? Had reaching the final round of the final been too much for her and she'd gone to pieces? She looked calm and confident enough sitting up there, but what was she feeling on the *inside*?

Graham Large was looking pretty pleased with himself as he sat at his keyboard, but he seemed to have every reason to. As far as Jackie could see, he'd only made two or three mistakes at most.

Malcolm walked back to the centre of the stage and thanked Hieronymus Peach for the final time as he popped the crocodile glove puppet into his valise and was cheered off the stage, waving to the audience. Malcolm then turned to the screens.

From where Le Fay was sitting, she could see the surprise on his face. He frowned again and looked at both screens carefully.

Feeling what he did about Le Fay and Graham Large, Malcolm didn't want to humiliate the young McNally girl in front of the audience by announcing the terrible number of mistakes she'd made in this, the final round. Instead, he went straight to the announcement.

'After local and regional heats, just four people made it to today's national Grand Final. Four people who can count themselves winners for just being up here on this stage today' – there were claps and cheers – 'but there can only be one runner-up and one champion. And the runner-up is . . . Le Fay McNally!'

The crowd cheered and Le Fay came to the front of the stage. She really thought she'd been in with a real chance of winning it. If only I hadn't made those few mistakes at the end, she thought. Whatever I think of Graham Lard as a person, he must be good at this, and deserves to win the competition.

Malcolm shook her warmly by the hand. 'Well done for being runner up, Le Fay,' he said. 'Let's have your family up here!'

Jackie, Joshua, Albie and Fergal didn't need asking twice. Le Fay might not have won, but they were all very proud of their sister. They all tried to hug her at once and Fergal, being the smallest, got pushed to the back and almost tripped over the spaghetti of wires, hidden behind a curtain, connecting all the computers, keyboards screens and lights.

Forever inquisitive, he realised how they 'switched off' one of the big screens above the stage when a contestant was eliminated. They simply pulled the particular cable jack plug from its socket. The two remaining screens – his sister Le Fay's and winner Graham Large's – were still plugged in: red jack plug into green socket and green jack plug into red.

Jackie was tugging him. Time to get off the stage with Le Fay holding the runner-up scroll.

When Graham Large went up to accept the winning prize from the chairman of Tap 'n' Type himself, Count Medoc Silverman, the whole front row of the audience leapt to their feet and clapped and cheered. Two photographers came forward, one from one of the Capital City's Leading

Evening Newspapers and another in an electric-blue suit.

Le Fay recognised him as the photographer working for the Large Lunches company magazine. Fergal recognised him as the electric-blue-coloured shape he'd seen lurking in the shadows after the power cut . . . lurking near where the wires were connecting the overhead screens to the computer. What had Fergal seen up onstage? A red jack plug in a green socket and a green jack plug in a red.

Then the blinding truth hit Fergal like a bolt of lightning (or like he would hit the pavement later on): the cables must be colour-coded. Green was supposed to go in green and red in red. The sockets had been switched in the so-called 'power cut', which meant that whatever Graham typed would appear on Le Fay's screen above the stage, and whatever she typed would appear on his!

All Graham Large would have had to do was type plenty of deliberate mistakes, which would appear on Le Fay's big screen as hers! He knew that she was good and would make very few mistakes, and that's what would appear on his screen. He was guaranteed to win, the cheat!

Fergal tugged at Jackie's arm and she leant towards him in her seat to hear what he had to say above the whoops and cheers of the Large family.

She had suspiciously good hearing for a mere human being. Her eyes widened in anger and amazement as she realised what her little brother was saying. But what should she do? She couldn't simply stand up and say: 'Cheat!' What if they were wrong? She couldn't be 100 per cent sure that the electric jack plugs and sockets were colour-coded.

Pushing her way past people in her row, with 'excuse me' after 'excuse me' as she banged against their knees, Jackie made it over to Mr Peach, who was standing in the side aisle. Fergal could see her explaining everything, with frantic hand gestures.

The next thing he knew, the ventriloquist had made his way up onstage and had disappeared behind the grinning Graham Large and his immediate family.

The room fell silent as Graham stepped forward and began his acceptance speech. 'The saying goes: "May the best man win,"' he sneered, 'and, as the only man, against three girls, you might think my winning a foregone conclusion–'

Just then there was a loud fizz and the two screens above them went blank, only to come to life again seconds later but with the badly spelled words on Large's screen and the ones with very few errors on Le Fay's.

There was a gasp, and muttering from the audience, and confusion on the stage, where they didn't know what was going on until, following the eyes of those below, they too turned to look up at the screens.

Malcolm Kent hurried back on to the stage. 'Ladies and gentlemen,' he said, grinning from ear to ear. 'I'm sorry to report that, owing to some confusion in the power cut, some misconnections were made, resulting in Master Graham Large's *twenty-six* typing and spelling errors' – he really emphasised the number – 'appearing on Miss McNally's screen by mistake. I therefore reverse the order of finalists and declare Le Fay McNally the rightful winner and Tap 'n' Type National Champion!'

He hadn't actually called Large a cheat, you'll notice – that's not good for business – but everyone knew what he meant. Everyone who wasn't a Large looked outraged and delighted both at once.

Before Le Fay knew what was happening, Jackie, Albie, Joshua, Anna Malting and her mum were carrying Le Fay shoulder high up the steps on to the stage.

Fergal's arms weren't long enough, but he (and Peggy Snoot) ran up with them. The disgraced Graham Large, meanwhile, was running offstage in the opposite direction, blubbing like a baby (but a very big one, old enough to know better).

Fergal felt a hand pat him on the shoulder. 'A nice piece of detective work, my boy,' said Mr Peach. 'Well done.'

Meanwhile, out in the foyer, a real detective was planning his next move. That was Twinkle-Toes Tweedy, of course, and he was about to haul Le Fay McNally off for questioning, in his linen closet of an office.

Chapter Ten

Captain Charlie 'Twinkle-Toes' Tweedy (retired), the chief house detective of The Dell hotel, was in a very good mood indeed. Housekeeper Mrs Launa Doon, had reported that – according to her 'girls' who had cleaned the rooms – only five rooms on the east side had been missing tissue boxes that morning. She gave him a list of the numbers.

It was a pretty safe bet, therefore (though admittedly not a 100-per-cent-watertight certainty), that one of the guests from one of these five rooms had used their box of tissues to wedge open the fire-escape door.

The detective took the list to the Reception desk and asked for details on the guests. Of the five rooms, three of the people had already checked out, which left two people to investigate on site. Of course, it was possible that the culprit had been one of the three who'd already left. It was also possible that it was one of the two remaining, so Tweedy would start with them. They were a Mr Norton Lisp in Room 1651 and a Miss Le Fay McNally in Room 1428. Next to Le Fay's name on her hotel registration card was written: 'minor'. This didn't mean that someone had wrongly recorded her profession as someone who dug for coal or tin or suchlike. *That* kind of miner is spelled with an 'e'. This kind of minor – with an 'o' – simply means that Le Fay was a child.

The card also said: 'In the care of Malcolm Kent, Tap 'n' Type competition.'

The cogs started whirring in Tweedy's brain. He'd met a little girl by the lifts who'd said that she was staying in the hotel and was in the typing competition. He'd also seen the back view of a girl – which could most definitely have been her – when he'd looked out of the fire exit wedged open with the tissues, alarm ringing. She'd been in the distance and walking ever so innocently, but it was the same girl. He was sure of it! He remembered having thought there was something familiar about the girl when she'd spoken those few words to him.

The detective was now convinced that Le Fay had been the one to wedge the door open. Call it a hunch. Call it a detective's intuition. Call it what you will. It wasn't a matter of having evidence or undeniable proof. It was a gut feeling, after years on the job, that he'd found the guilty party.

But guilty of what? Wedging a door open. But why? To let someone sneak in the back way, of course. Tweedy made his way to Room 1428 and knocked on the door. There was no reply. He knocked again. Still no reply.

He pulled a large key out of his pocket. This was the master key. This key was what's called a skeleton key. It could open every locked door in The Dell. The chief house detective slipped it into the keyhole of Le Fay's room, turned it and walked inside.

The maid had been and made the bed, cleaned the bedroom and bathroom, changed the towels and replaced the missing box of tissues but, if there were still clues to be found, old Twinkle-Toes Tweedy would find them . . .

Some ten minutes later, the only strange thing he'd discovered was some strands of animal hair on the curtains at waist height. They were thick, like a dog's. Had the girl smuggled a huge pet into her room? Was that what all this had been about? But where was it now?

Tweedy picked up the phone and dialled '1'.

'Room Service,' said a cheery voice.

Tweedy explained who he was and asked what, if anything, had been ordered for the room since Le Fay McNally had checked in. He was told about the chicken sandwich and the hot chocolate and the large piece of fish with extra chips – all in the same day, when Tweedy knew jolly well that the competition included a finger buffet and supper.

Back downstairs, some fifteen minutes later, he talked with the waiters and waitresses who'd served dinner in the Sizzle Grill and soon learnt that Le Fay had taken a doggy bag of leftovers up to her room after the meal! There was no way she could have eaten all that food herself! A hungry dog, however, would have wolfed it down.

Tweedy was now sure that he'd almost solved the case – but for a few important details. Le Fay hadn't had the pet with her when he'd seen her back view in the street. She'd obviously planned to wedge open the fire escape and then come back with the dog, except that the alarm had gone off and the exit had been closed. How, then, had she finally managed to get the beast up to her room? That was the real puzzle. The hairs on the curtains and the amount of food ordered and eaten proved that she must have hidden and fed the creature . . . but where was it now?

These were the two questions that Twinkle-Toes wanted the answers to more than anything else, but they could be easily answered. Now he knew who the culprit was and what she was up to, he could simply confront her and get her to tell him.

Admittedly, smuggling a pet into one of The Dell's bedrooms wasn't the worst crime that had been committed in the hotel. It wasn't as if the girl was letting a whole bunch of people stay in her room without paying, or stealing anything . . . it was just that Charlie 'Twinkle-Toes' Tweedy didn't like anything to be going on in his hotel that shouldn't be going on. And now he was ready to confront the culprit . . .

*

With the National Championships of the Tap 'n' Type competition at an end, the doors to the Empress Conference Suite burst open and the National Champion – a certain Le Fay McNally – was whisked into the foyer on a sea of shoulders.

As the double swing doors swung open and the

people poured out, the chief house detective's eyes widened at the sight of them.

He recognised Malcolm Kent as one of the organisers and Mr Peach as the well-known beat poet and ventriloquist . . . and there was no mistaking Le Fay, though she looked a lot happier than when he'd spoken to her by the lifts. She was radiating happiness, beaming with pride and bursting with joy all at once. She was giving off so much heat that she'd have melted a snowman at ten paces. (Not that snowmen or women were allowed in The Dell unless, of course, they had a reservation.)

But it was the McNally family as a whole that struck Charlie Tweedy like a slap on the back: those red freckles, the sticky-out ears, the red wiry hair and the buck teeth . . . Surely they couldn't be? They *couldn't* be . . . but they looked so much like him, they *must* be! That's why little Le Fay had looked so familiar when he'd first laid eyes on her. They must be Rufus McNally's family. His children! McNally was a common enough name, but with those features? There was no doubt about it!

The chief house detective gasped and, for the first time in all his years at The Dell, he forgot his duty. He forgot that he should be questioning Le Fay about smuggling an animal up into her room, against hotel policy. Instead, he simply wanted to WHOOP with delight. So that's exactly what he did – and he broke out into a little dance on his tippy-tippy-toes. For a big man, he danced with great elegance, which was a strange sight indeed, made even stranger by the fact that he had the broadest grin he could fit on his face without planning permission. It was BIG.

Anyone who'd just walked into the foyer of The Dell off the street would have been in for a surprise. The Large family were leaving en masse (which is French for 'in one big lump', which is appropriate when you consider who we're talking about). Graham's dad, David Large of Large Lunches kept on slapping the back of his son's neck and calling him a cheat. Various other relatives were shuffling out, shamefaced with their eyes to the ground, whilst Mrs Large was bossing around some poor man carrying all their boy's luggage.

Le Fay, meanwhile, was still being carried shoulder-high around the foyer in a lap of honour, watched enthusiastically by everyone from Malcolm and Mr Peach to the Maltings and the Snoops.

And then there was Twinkle-Toes Tweedy doing his dance of pure, unadulterated happiness.

If this were a film, I might end it here, with the

camera pulling away from the action, up and out of the doors and away past the outside of The Dell. Because this isn't a film, the receptionist picked up a phone and called the duty manager.

'I need you in Reception,' he said. 'There're some weird things going on!'

Now I think I'd be failing in my duty as the narrator of these unlikely exploits if I didn't take the time or trouble to explain why Twinkle-Toes Tweedy was dancing with delight at having come face to face with Rufus McNally's five children: Jackie, Albie, Joshua, Le Fay and Fergal. Most of you will remember that he was a retired policeman, but some of you will also remember that, way, way back on page 27, I said that he was an ex-naval man. To put it another way, he'd once been in the navy. I also mentioned on page 5 that the McNally's dad – back in the days before he was bitter, sick and twisted – had, on three occasions, 'done heroic deeds to save others trapped as their vessels went down'. As a young sailor, long, long before he'd even joined the police department and become a detective, Able Seaman Charlie Tweedy had been one of those people Captain Rufus McNally had saved.

Tweedy had been trapped in the galley of a ship torpedoed by the Enemy with a capital 'E'. A ship's galley is its kitchen, and a huge stove had blocked Tweedy's only possible exit as the galley began to fill with water. Tweedy had known then that he was going to die. He was young and fighting to protect the freedom of his country, but he hadn't expected it to end like this: in a kitchen filling up with pounding seawater. Then Captain Rufus had appeared like some comic-book hero. This was Rufus McNally before he lost his leg. This was Rufus McNally the highly decorated ship's captain who never lost a man if he could help it. At great personal risk to himself, he'd made his way through the *Mary-Jane* and had already freed and rescued a number of other sailors before reaching Tweedy in the galley.

What's all the more brave was that this wasn't even Rufus McNally's vessel. He'd boarded the *Mary-Jane* when the ship had been hit and its captain hadn't answered his radio messages. A captain often went down with his own ship. Rufus McNally was risking going down in another man's.

Well, the very fact that Twinkle-Toes Tweedy was dancing in the foyer of The Dell hotel all those years later shows that the McNally's dad had somehow rescued Able Seaman Tweedy from the galley. He'd used every last ounce of his considerable strength and a crowbar to move that stove and get him out just in time.

There had never been time for proper 'thank yous'. Neither man had been badly injured and both had been back on active duty in a matter of days, but Tweedy had never forgotten the strange-looking Captain McNally with his wiry and unmanageable hair, freckles, and buck teeth.

When the war was done, he had gone out of his way to track down McNally to thank him personally. The Naval Office wouldn't give out his address, but had forwarded Tweedy's letters to Rufus who – now with one leg, and hate in his heart – had never even bothered to read them. He would have torn them up if his wife hadn't returned them unopened, out of politeness.

Although Tweedy had stopped actively trying to track down McNally (and, out of respect, he'd never abused his power as a policeman to find out from official records, not available to the public, where his saviour lived) he'd often wondered whether Rufus McNally had a family or what he was doing now . . . and, all these years later, Charlie 'Twinkle-Toes' Tweedy had absolutely no doubt that these were the man's children in front of him now.

Chapter Eleven

Back in Room 1428, the celebrations were still under way. Le Fay was a hero for having won the competition and Fergal was a hero for having exposed the cheat. In all the excitement, they'd forgotten about the prize itself, until Jackie caught sight of the golden envelope sticking out of the pocket in Le Fay's dress.

'Go on, Le Fay. Open it!' she said.

Le Fay opened it. Inside was a voucher for a very expensive, state-of-the-art, top-of-the-range computer with every conceivable attachment and gizmo: printer, scanner, camera – you name it, it had it.

'"Exchangeable at any electrical or computer store",' Le Fay read, her eyes widening in wonder. Then she looked a little sad. 'Of course, we must collect the computer and then sell it,' she said.

'Yeah!' said Albie excitedly. 'Think of all the

shopping we can get with that –'

'The repairs we can do to the apartment –' said Joshua.

'We could feed Smoky every day so she doesn't have to catch rats –' said Le Fay.

'We could live off the money from selling the computer for ages,' said Fergal.

'No,' said Jackie.

'No? What do you mean "no"?' demanded Albie.

'I mean that Le Fay won the computer so she gets to keep the computer,' said Jackie, quietly.

'We could always sell the computer and buy a cheaper one along with all the other stuff we need,' said Le Fay.

'No,' said Jackie. 'You won it. You deserve it and – who knows? – we might even find a way of you making money with this fabulous computer and your keyboard skills.'

Le Fay threw her arms around her big sister and gave her a hug. 'Thank you!' she cried.

Albie was about to protest, until Jackie gave him one of her no-nonsense stares over Le Fay's shoulder. He knew when he was beaten.

There was a knock at the door.

'Who is it?' asked Le Fay. She and the others half-expected it to be Malcolm Kent, who'd been so nice to them from the word go.

When the person the other side of the door announced himself to be 'Charlie Tweedy', it threw Le Fay into an unnecessary panic.

'It's the chief house detective!' she hissed.

If any of them had stopped to think rationally for one minute, it would have occurred to them that they could have pretended to have all gone up to the room at the end of the competition to celebrate. No one need know that they planned to spend one last night in it. But Le Fay had told them about her meeting with Captain Tweedy, and they'd all witnessed the very strange way he'd behaved in the foyer earlier . . . and Le Fay's irrational panic was contagious. Albie and Joshua ran straight for the bathroom at the same time and became briefly wedged together in the doorway. Jackie snatched up what evidence there was of their being in the room and was about to head into the bathroom too, when she saw Fergal leaning out of the window.

Le Fay later said that she thought Fergal might have been looking to see if there was an outer ledge that he could step out on to and hide.

Whatever his reason, Jackie turned and cried, 'Don't lean out of that window!'

But, as we all know from hindsight, it was too late. Fergal fell. Jackie dashed across the room and leant out, grabbing at thin air. She let out a pained cry of 'No!' stretching the 'o' to last a good fifteen seconds. What I neglected to mention before was that the cry turned into a howl and, by the time the remaining McNallys had thrown open the door, streaming past a startled Twinkle-Toes Tweedy – who'd heard the howl and had no idea what was going on – Jackie had turned into a jackal.

Why else do you think I said that there was more to Jackie's nickname 'Jackal' than her snapping and snarling, back on page 7?

Why else would she – a grown woman – have to 'jump up' to press the 'down' button at the lifts, on page 23? Who else do you think was the furry creature shown in the wonderful illustration on the same page? (Look between those running legs.) Who else could have left thick dog-like hairs on Le Fay's curtains? And what about Jackie's 'suspiciously good hearing for a mere human', I mention on page 109? Well, it's because she *was* no mere human, of course!

A shame none of the others had Jackie's amazing abilities, though that's not to say that they won't turn out to have some very distinct ones of their own. (Their late mother named them for specific reasons. The clues are there.) There are three books in this series and something has to happen in the other two! If Fergal had been able to turn into a golden eagle, or even a hedgehog with a parachute, things might have turned out very differently indeed!

And think how Captain Charlie 'Twinkle-Toes' Tweedy felt when he later pieced together what had happened (though, fortunately, he didn't realise that the 'dog' he'd seen dashing from the room and the big sister weeping by her dead brother were, in truth, one and the same).

He'd come to Room 1428 to share in the good news and delight at having come across them after all these years – the children of the man who'd saved his life as a young sailor – and in the process he'd indirectly led to one of them falling to his death . . . which wasn't the best way to say thank you.

Captain Tweedy was beside himself with mixed measures of grief, guilt and anguish. The only thing stopping him from falling to pieces was being strong for Jackie, Albie, Joshua and Le Fay. Someone else who was brilliant in that role was Malcolm Kent of Tap 'n' Type. I have to say that he's a person I'd be greatly honoured to call a friend.

Much of the rest you know. Fergal was taken to the morgue at the Sacred Heart Hospital, while Tweedy, Malcolm and the management of The Dell did what they could to comfort the McNallys.

'Should I ring your father?' said Malcolm, who hadn't found a contact number in Le Fay's competition file.

'We don't have a phone at home,' said Jackie. 'And I don't want anyone else going around telling him.'

In the end, they all went home that night. The Dell had a minibus they used for staff outings and special occasions. It had never been sent on such a sad mission before. Charlie Tweedy drove, Jackie gave directions and Malcolm sat with Joshua, Albie and Le Fay, the forgotten computer voucher crumpled in the golden envelope in her pocket.

Does some good come out of tragedy? In this case, I'm pleased to report, yes. The fall of Fergal certainly made a better man of Captain Rufus McNally. He cried at the news in a way that startled all his remaining children. They'd expected him to bottle up his grief like his anger, and to take it out on them and the bottles; but he sobbed floods of tears and – as they were to discover over the following weeks – those tears did much to wash away his bitterness, sickness and twistedness. He became much more the man he'd once been before collecting all those bottles. He became the kind of man Tweedy recognised as the person who'd saved him all those years before. Sure, he'd lost a leg and gained a big red nose, but this was the guy who'd risked his life so many times to save others. He even tore up the note from his doctor that said he was 'excused parenting'.

The two captains – one a retired sea captain and the other a retired police captain – became firm friends. Malcolm became a close friend of Jackie and the children. He became close enough to learn Jackie's secret that she could become a jackal, and the secrets of Albie, Joshua and Le Fay, as they themselves discovered them. They never forgot Fergal, of course, but not for the reasons you might think . . .

*

For some reason it was important for the pathologist to weigh Fergal's brain – perhaps to work out how much of it had slopped out of the boy's ears, nose, throat (and perhaps the odd eye socket or two). Unfortunately, the scales had broken when, during his lunch hour, Dennis, the assistant path lab assistant – whose usual summer job was selling ice cream, remember? – had tried to weigh his bull terrier in them, while the boss was out.

So what should Dennis do until they were fixed? He decided to pop Fergal's brain in one of the large jars he'd seen on the draining board by the huge stainless-steel sinks running along one wall of the morgue.

He picked up the brain with his gloved hands and glooped it into a jar. It reminded Dennis of an overcooked cauliflower. Now all he needed to do was to add some of that preserving liquid – what was it called? Formaldehyde, that was it – so that it'd stay in one piece until the scales were fixed and his boss could weigh it. Dennis was sure that his boss would be proud of his quick thinking and, as a result, wouldn't be quite so annoyed that Dennis had not only broken the special scales, but had got dog hairs everywhere in the first place!

The problem was that there wasn't a drop of formaldehyde to be found. Muttering under his breath, Dennis dashed out of the basement entrance of the hospital, up some stairs littered with ancient leaves from previous autumns, now dry and skeletal, and across the street. A few blocks down, he reached MA'S PICKLING STORE, along the bottom of the store sign of which was written: 'For All Your Pickling Needs'. He hurried inside and had little time to exchange pleasantries with 'Ma' who was, if the truth be told, Mrs Bloinstein, a friend of Dennis's Aunt Patty, and would no doubt report to her that her nephew, Dennis, had come to her store during his hospital working hours to buy a gallon of pickling vinegar.

Dennis dashed back down the street, across the road, down the steps and into the Sacred Heart Hospital's basement morgue, carrying the plastic gallon bottle of pickling vinegar as fast as his legs could carry him. He'd poured it into the jar containing Fergal's brain, and just fitted the tight-seal lid, when a man in a white coat appeared, wheeling a trolley stacked with store supplies.

'Hi, Dennis,' he said. 'No one else around?'

'No,' panted Dennis.

'Then you'll have to sign for this. A fresh supply of formaldehyde. OK?'

'OK,' said Dennis snatching the pen and signing.

The guy in the white coat wondered why Dennis was glaring at him as he piled the bottles of formaldehyde on to a wooden workbench. What had he done to upset him? He sniffed the air. 'Do I smell vinegar?' he asked.

'Don't be crazy,' said Dennis, handing him back the clipboard and pen. 'Who'd be mad enough to eat anything in here, what with all these bodies around?'

'True,' nodded the man. 'Hey, what happened to those scales?'

'Don't ask,' sighed Dennis.

That night, when the small, masked burglar broke into the morgue of the Sacred Heart Hospital he was very disappointed. He had hoped to find row upon row of jars of human brains to choose from. There were always row upon row of brains in

Frankenstein movies when the scientist's assistant Igor broke into the place, so why not here?

All the small, masked burglar could find was one. It was labelled:

FERGAL MCNALLY,
JUVENILE.

and had a slight whiff of pickling vinegar about it.

'It'll have to do,' muttered the small, masked burglar to himself (which is convenient for us). 'I only hope that the master is pleased.'

With that, he stuffed the jar containing Fergal's brain under his jumper, and hurried out into the night, heading for Fishbone Forest. The ground rumbled beneath him. 'Oh no! Not another hole,' he muttered . . .

Which was all very unlikely indeed, wasn't it?

THE END
of the first exploit

Epilogue

'Philip!'

What?

'*Is that really the end?*'

It says so, doesn't it?

'*But does it have to end here?*'

Every story has to end somewhere.

'*But here?*'

Here's as good as any place. Everything's rather neatly tied up, if the truth be told.

'*But what happened next?*'

Would you settle for: "And they all lived happily ever after."?

'*It's rather unlikely, isn't it? Especially if Fergal isn't living at all . . . And who's the small burglar, and who's his master?*'

Good point. I suggest you read 'Unlikely Exploits 2: Heir of Mystery.'

'*I didn't know you'd written a sequel.*'

That's because I haven't.

'*You haven't?*'

I haven't.

'*Then . . .?*'

Yet.

The Philip Ardagh Club